Darcy's Royal Dilemma

Barbara Silkstone

Thanks to Jane Austen for sharing her
timeless, beloved characters.

And

Very special thanks to Vanessa J. for her
brilliant ideas. I am very proud of her!

PROLOGUE

It is a truth universally acknowledged that a single man in possession of a mysterious box must be in want of a witch.

The Netherfield footman carefully unloaded Darcy's and Bingley's baggage. The friends traveled lightly with only one small trunk each, having left London in a rush. Darcy held a small jewelry box close to his chest. Looking about, he tucked the container under his swirling black cape and bounded into Netherfield mansion as if being pursued.

CHAPTER ONE
LONGBOURN

"My dear Mr. Bennet," said Mrs. Bennet one fine day, "Have you heard that Netherfield Park is let at last?"

Mr. Bennet looked up from his book long enough to inform his wife that he had not. And then returned to reading the book he had read many times before; in fact he knew it by heart. It was the book he hid behind whenever Mrs. Bennet began to chatter.

Mrs. Bennet was not known for her patience. "Do you not want to know who has let Netherfield Park?"

He turned his book over in his lap and studied his wife of twenty plus years. "I have no objection to you telling me."

The level of her excitement was such that her words came out in a shrill chirp. "A young man of large fortune from London. He came down on Monday in a chaise and four to see the place and took it then and there. His servants are arriving as we speak."

Mr. Bennet cast her an impassive look. "As *you* speak my dear, for I have had no opportunity." Watching his wife clap her hands and flutter about the room, he longed for a swatter to bring her down.

"I am told he is single!" She twittered. "A single man of large fortune; four or five thousand a year. What a fine thing for our girls! Mr. Bennet, you must pay a call on our new neighbor!"

"You and the girls may go, or send them by themselves, which would be still better, for you are as handsome as any of your daughters. The gentleman may like you the best of the party," he teased.

Mrs. Bennet fanned herself, flustered at his compliment and not recognizing the jest in his words. "When a woman has five grown daughters, she gives up thinking of her own beauty. I have not much beauty to think of; at least not until all five are married off. But you, Mr. Bennet, must go and pay a visit to our new neighbor as soon as possible; there will be a great rush for his attentions."

He turned over his book and took to reading again, without glancing up at her. "I do not have the time."

"But consider your daughters. It would be ideal for one to marry such an eligible man and to live so close to Longbourn. How can you deny them or me? Sir William and Lady Lucas are determined to go. You know they visit no newcomers, but in this case they are resolute. If you do not make the first call, then it will be impossible for us to visit him."

When Mr. Bennet did not look up, she continued to prattle unaware of the smirk that graced his face. He enjoyed nothing more than playfully baiting her, for it had become the style between them.

"I dare say the gentleman would take pleasure in meeting you," Mr. Bennet said. "As their mother you can carry a letter from me in which I will assure him that I would not object to his marrying whichever of our daughters he might choose. Although, I would throw in a good word for Lizzy."

Fanny Bennet's mouth dropped open like a fish gasping for breath. "You will do no such thing. Lizzy is not a bit better than the others; she is not half so handsome as Jane, nor half so cheerful as Lydia. I am put off that you are always giving Lizzy preference."

He closed his book, placing his hands one upon the other. "Let me share with you what you refuse to see. Your girls are silly and ignorant like other girls, but Lizzy and Jane have something more of a quickness than their sisters."

"Thomas Bennet, how can you be so unkind as to demean your own children? You do this merely to vex me. You know my nerves are not good."

"My dear, have I not always said your nerves are of the best quality? You possess the highest strung nerves of any lady in Hertfordshire."

CHAPTER TWO
DINNER THE FOLLOWING EVENING

Observing his second daughter wearing a new dress at dinner, Mr. Bennet said, "Lizzy, I hope Mr. Bingley will like that lovely dress for it certainly brings out the sparkle in your eyes."

"Of whom do you speak?" Mrs. Bennet chirped. "Who is this Mr. Bingley?"

"That is the name of our neighbor," her husband said, without looking up from his plate.

Mrs. Bennet snorted a very unladylike snort. "We will never know what this Mr. Bingley likes since we are not to visit."

Seeking to calm her mother, Elizabeth said, "We shall come to meet the man, perhaps at the assemblies. Mrs. Long has promised to introduce him."

Mrs. Bennet repeated her snort, this time louder. "Mrs. Long has two nieces of her own. She is of a selfish and hypocritical nature, and will put her own before this Mr. Bingley with no thought for our family. None at all."

"When is your next ball to be, Lizzy?" Mr. Bennet said.

"In a fortnight," she said, pleased to change the subject from Mrs. Long.

"Then, Mrs. Bennet, you shall have the pleasure of introducing Mr. Bingley to Mrs. Long at the ball."

"But that is impossible! You vex me so!" she said, clattering her fork onto her plate. "Impossible when I will never make his acquaintance," she pouted. "Not until he has married one of Mrs. Long's nieces."

Still not looking up from his plate, Thomas Bennet continued to tease his wife. "If you will not present him, then I shall introduce him to Mrs. Long, but first to our daughters. For I have found him to be quite amenable," said Mr. Bennet, enjoying his bantering.

Mrs. Bennet and all five Bennet sisters were stunned to hear their father had met with the gentleman from Netherfield as he had been so adamant in his refusal to greet their new neighbor. Such was his mocking nature that Mr. Bennet would pretend to be of one mind and yet do the exact opposite.

He continued in a most casual manner while holding the rapt attention of the women. "Bingley is the family name. The gentleman is single and maintains a large home in London, but he is seeking a country home as well. Mr. Charles Bingley has leased Netherfield with the intention of experiencing rural conviviality."

"Why then, he is quite perfect!" Mrs. Bennet almost swooned with delight. "To have one of our daughters married to him and living so close."

"In my opinion the man is a bit too amenable." He knit his fingers as if contemplating how best to phrase his next disclosure. "Mr. Bingley is joined in his visit by a gentleman friend. This friend, Mr. Fitzwilliam Darcy does not appear in the least affable, but rather aloof and agitated."

Mrs. Bennet continued to hunt for loose threads. "Do you think the gentlemen are both men of means?" she could barely speak for her excitement and finally smacked her hands palms down on the table beside her plate. "Why did you not tell me of your visit to Netherfield?"

"I had not intended to call on him this morning, and yet no sooner had I mounted my horse bound for Meryton, when I found myself at Netherfield Park. And no, I had not imbibed even a small sip of brandy to account for my misdirection."

Elizabeth caught Jane wearing a cat-that-ate-the-canary smile. Had father's excursion to greet the new neighbor been at her sister's bidding? Elizabeth raised her brows, and smiled, her dimple giving away her thoughts.

Jane blushed and looked away.

"I only just stayed the required time and no longer, for I felt Mr. Bingley to be a cordial fellow, but anxious for my departure."

Mrs. Bennet flapped her hands in the air as if she were about to take flight. "I am so excited!"

Ignoring his wife's chirping, Mr. Bennet continued, "This Darcy chap was even more on edge. Not as much a victim of his nerves as yourself, Mrs. Bennet, but nonetheless, quite anxious. It is hard to put into words but there's something odd there. Perhaps travel does not agree with them, although they gave me to understand they had only come from London, so the journey was not a long distance." Mr. Bennet stabbed a chunk of juicy meat, popped it into his mouth, and moaned softly as he chewed.

"How good it was of you, Mr. Bennet! But I knew I should persuade you at last. You have done the right thing for your daughters. I am sure very soon we shall have our first son-in-law. I am so pleased."

Mr. Bennet winked at Elizabeth while Mrs. Bennet continued to waffle on. "It is such a good joke that you should have gone and never said a word about it until now."

"I have a feeling that Mr. Bingley will prove to be a lovely man," Jane said, in that misty otherworldly way of hers that Elizabeth so admired.

Mrs. Bennet picked up the thread of the conversation. "I would assume they will be paying us a visit within the next few days, as courtesy dictates? Surely you mentioned our five pretty daughters?"

Mr. Bennet nodded as he reached for his wine glass. "I believe I did."

"How glorious!" Mrs. Bennet said as she clapped her hands, her rings catching the light from the candles. "If I can see one of my daughters happily settled at Netherfield, and the other four equally well married, I shall have nothing more to wish for."

CHAPTER THREE
DARCY AND BINGLEY VISIT

Within two days, Mr. Bingley and Mr. Darcy returned Mr. Bennet's visit. The gentlemen sat all of ten minutes with him in his study. Mr. Bingley peeped over his shoulder at the slightest sound as if waiting for someone special to tiptoe into the room. His talents were set most sensitively, for he knew someone wonderful was about to enter his life.

Mrs. Bennet could no longer contain herself and popped uninvited into her husband's study, setting the stage for how both Mr. Bingley and Mr. Darcy would forever perceive her—meddlesome and intrusive.

Wearing her best morning dress, with gemstone earrings dangling from under her cap, and a huge ring on each hand, she took a quick assessment of Bingley and Darcy. Warming immediately to the former and sensing what she perceived to be persnicketies on the part of the latter, she responded kindly to one and in a most hostile manner to the other.

Jane and Elizabeth stood outside the study, peering through the wedge between the doorframe and the door. A sigh escaped Bingley's lips as he sensed Jane's presence. Before Elizabeth could restrain her sister, Jane dashed into the room. Elizabeth followed.

At first startled and then a bit amused at Jane's forwardness, Mr. Bennet introduced his two eldest daughters. The introduction was brief; Darcy behaved as if he were afraid he would contract a sickness from Mrs. Bennet. Standoffish, Darcy barely made eye contact with Jane or Elizabeth.

Charles Bingley greeted Elizabeth graciously and then immediately fell under Jane's spell, stumbling over his words, his unblinking eyes as large as two robin's eggs.

No sooner had the visitors made the sisters' acquaintance, than Darcy pulled out his pocket watch, glanced at the time, and remarked to Mr. Bingley that they must be on their way. Darcy's agitation increased as Bingley savored longing glances at Jane while delaying their exit.

Desperate to launch her daughters into Mr. Bingley's path before he escaped, Mrs. Bennet recommended the Meryton Assembly to be the best way to meet the residents of Hertfordshire. Mr.

Bingley responded with delight, claiming a great love for dancing. He exchanged looks with Jane and she smiled demurely.

"The ball shall be held in less than a fortnight. But that is much too long to wait for the pleasure of conversation with new friends. Please honor us with your company for supper on Saturday..." She hesitated, "...and you Mr. Darcy?" her reluctant invitation to Bingley's friend hung dead in the air.

Fanny Bennet's mind was racing like a Christmas goose avoiding the axe. The moment she uttered the invitation to dinner, she was already planning the courses that would do credit to her housekeeping and so reflect positively on her daughters.

"I would be quite honored to accept," Bingley said. He turned to Darcy for his acceptance and then faltered as glancing at Darcy's stormy countenance reminded him of yet another complication. "I am afraid I must decline," Bingley said. "I have promised to accompany my sisters from London to Netherfield. I am to depart on Friday for London to escort them for an extended visit to my new home."

In the two minutes she had taken to issue the invitation, Mrs. Bennet had already planned the entire meal. Elizabeth imagined she could hear her mother's face clank to the floor in a pout when she realized the dinner would not occur. Her nerves did not handle disappointment well.

Bingley felt obliged to explain. "My younger sister, Caroline Bingley, currently resides in London with my married sister and her husband, Mr. and Mrs. Hurst. They have expressed a wish to see Netherfield. My apologies but I...we...must decline your kind invitation." He appeared truly dismayed. "May we look forward to seeing you all at the Meryton Assembly? I know my sisters would take great delight in meeting members of Hertfordshire society."

Mrs. Bennet was quite disconcerted to have lost the opportunity to attach herself to Mr. Bingley. She determined to make the most of the upcoming ball with the greatest of confidence that Mr. Bingley would commit his affections to one of her daughters before that day was done. She would consider nothing less.

CHAPTER FOUR
NETHERFIELD

"I thought you had refused your family's request to join us. Our stay at Netherfield is not a holiday!" Darcy snapped under his breath as he took his stallion's reins from the Bennets' footman. "Caroline is like a grain of sand in my eye. She is both irritating and difficult to remove. Bringing her close to what we have wrought could present more problems."

Bingley cast him an equally testy look as he mounted his horse. "*I* have not wrought. *You* have wrought. *You* are the wroughter," he said, cautious not to let the servant hear him.

Matching his friend's defiant glare, Darcy settled in Parsifal's saddle. The events of the last few days seemed to be slipping from his control.

The men urged their horses into a canter and had soon put some distance between themselves and Longbourn manor. It was only then that Darcy felt comfortable in responding to Bingley's accusation.

"I admit it was all my error," Darcy said. "But if you wish to help me, please keep your sister at a distance until we have met with the hermit called Herman, and he has undone the wrong I have wrought."

"I will do my best. But much like you, Caroline is not easily governed. As to inviting her to stay on at Netherfield, I have decided I may wish to settle there and some tolerance may be required from you if you are to reside with me until your problem is resolved."

Darcy reined in his horse and sat staring at Bingley, not trusting himself to speak. London was where Darcy could best apply his powers. He took pleasure in the politics that drove Britain to be the foremost empire in the world. If he occasionally desired the life of a country squire, he had only to spend time at his estate in Derbyshire. But it was in London where Darcy felt he could save England from the machinations of the French. His every intention was for the good of king and country; he sought no personal gain. But he did require Bingley to be at his assistance in London in order to further his work there.

Bingley shrugged and then responded happily, "Hertfordshire is growing on me."

"It is not the shire that is growing on you, but rather a pair of blue eyes and a constant smile."

"If I take permanent residence here, the running of my household will require a mistress," Bingley said. "Caroline will be most eager to play the part, particularly if you are to be in attendance."

Darcy felt his throat constrict. This entire debacle had become a muddy bog into which he felt himself sinking like a rock. "Netherfield seemed the ideal place to lodge while we seek help with our problem. I did not think we would be setting up housekeeping."

"Not *our* problem but rather *your* problem. I am your friend until the end, but your ego created this cockup. Since what you have done has never been done before, I doubt a penalty has yet been created to match your crime. Perhaps you should consider emigrating to America? Although I understand they are much less tolerant of —"

"Let us not talk of this anymore. I am bored to death with catching flies," Darcy said, kicking Parsifal into a full gallop.

CHAPTER FIVE
THE MERYTON ASSEMBLY

All in attendance drew silent as the Bingley party entered the assembly room. Mr. Charles Bingley accompanied his two sisters: the younger, Caroline, dressed in a vivid orange dress that fought with the shades of her purple-red hair, Mrs. Louisa Hurst, the elder sister, in a peacock green and blue gown with tiny gems imbedded in the silken fabric—much too overdone for a country ball.

Mr. Hurst appeared as bland as any middle-aged gentleman being forced to attend an assembly when he would rather be at home lounging on his sofa. Mr. Darcy followed the party; he appeared elegant in his rich blue coat, tan brocade vest, and a perfect white cravat at this neck.

Mr. Bingley, dressed in the latest fashion for gentlemen of the ton, was instantly accepted for his pleasant countenance and unaffected manners. He had a ready smile for all he encountered and evidenced delight in each new introduction.

His sisters shared a haughty attitude, but were forgiven their pompous pretentions for they were ladies of fashion.

It was Mr. Darcy who drew the attention of the room with his fine, tall person, handsome features, and noble carriage. The gossips, for there were many, soon shared the delicious news that he was possessed of ten thousand a year. How they knew this within days of his arrival was part of the enchantment of Meryton— news in the small town moved faster than a bee's wings.

Mr. Bingley mingled throughout the assembly making the acquaintance of all the principal people in the room. It was evident by his beaming smile and lively carriage that he enjoyed balls. He danced most every dance and was conversant in a reserved, yet comfortable way with each of the young ladies whose mothers hung on his every smile and strained to read his lips from the distance of their seats.

But, above all, Bingley's eyes repeatedly found their way to Jane's elegant form as she danced with other men. He would have loved to dance more than the proper two dances with the blonde angel, but more than two would be tantamount to a proposal of marriage, and for that he was not yet ready.

The contrast between the gentlemen newcomers was as black is to white. Mr. Darcy danced only one dance with Mrs. Hurst and one with Miss Bingley. He behaved the total nob, declining introductions to any other lady. He stalked the room like a rooster in a chicken yard, demonstrating his boredom; he made no attempt to disguise his disgust with what he clearly perceived to be a lesser society.

Darcy occasionally spoke to one or the other of his party, but by his stance and snobbery made it quite clear he was the proudest, most disagreeable man to visit Meryton since the Norman Conquest.

Elizabeth watched Caroline Bingley with amused curiosity, for she discerned the woman was possessed of both shifty eyes and a sniffy nose. Elizabeth shared her thoughts with Jane who stood at her side, "Mother will not care for Miss Bingley, you can be assured."

"Miss Bingley? Why she is quite lovely. Vivacious would be the word I would use to describe her," Jane said, ever so sweetly.

Elizabeth thought vacuous more appropriate but she bit her tongue, took a chair, and sat out two dances due to the scarcity of young men. Uncomfortable at being a wallflower, her feelings were rendered all the more painful as Mr. Darcy stood near her. She attempted to appear at ease with her situation and smiled gaily as her sisters danced and flirted.

Mr. Bingley approached Darcy and encouraged him to dance as there was an obvious shortage of men, and a number of the young ladies were obliged to sit the dances out.

"I must have you dance," Bingley said to Darcy. "I hate to see you standing about in this stupid manner. Your behavior reflects poorly on you, and in turn on me."

Darcy all but snarled. "I will not, for you know how I detest dancing with strangers. It is false to place a smile on my face and pretend I am enjoying myself, as some simpering twit touches her fingers to mine and imagines herself becoming my wife."

"With very little effort you are able to be thoroughly obnoxious. If you puff up any more, you shall burst," Bingley said. "For someone who has just managed to cockup the line of succession to the throne, you remain quite full of yourself. Now ask a lady to dance before you become the most detested man in this room, for you can clearly see an abundance of delightful females and a shortage of gentlemen."

"And at such an assemblage as this there is not a woman in the room whom it would not be a punishment to me to stand up with," Darcy said.

"You have no one to blame but yourself for our being here," Bingley said. "Now please make an attempt to enjoy yourself, or at the least be sociable. These are good, gentle country people and very welcoming."

"They are only welcoming because these mother hens see us as wealthy husbands for their bimble-headed daughters," Darcy said. "Not one young lady here could carry on an intelligent conversation."

"Have you even attempted to carry on a conversation with one of the ladies? Elizabeth Bennet seems to possess a clever wit. Go speak with her."

"If Miss Elizabeth Bennet has said something clever, it has eluded me. Were I to speak two words, her mother would set upon me like a fly on honey. Speaking of flies, we must get back to Netherfield."

"You do go out of your way to dislike people. Yes, you have a problem to sort out, but that is not the fault of the people gathered here, but rather a fault of your own ego. There are times when you are ruled by that little devil that sits on your shoulder and tells you there is no feat you cannot accomplish."

Darcy sniffed before he spoke for he did not like having his ego attacked. "I imagine the Bennet you fancy has not stopped smiling long enough to utter a single word. How can she keep that perpetual smile on her face without developing a cramp in her cheeks?"

"You are being absolutely vile. You brought this adventure upon yourself. Now do not ruin this lovely evening for all in attendance. Allow the ladies a peek at the real charms of Fitzwilliam Darcy, for I know they are in there somewhere."

Bingley glanced at Jane; and she rewarded his look with a smile. "I am forever thankful I am not you. For you miss out on so many of life's joys with your rules of superiority," Bingley said. "Look about you! I have never met with so many pleasant girls in my life as I have this evening." He bobbed his head in the direction of the dance floor. "Several of them are uncommonly pretty."

Darcy quirked his lips before he spoke, "You are dancing with the only handsome girl in the room." He nodded towards Jane Bennet. "Once again you have committed your heart before consulting your head."

Bingley grinned and his eyes sparkled. "She is the most beautiful creature I have ever beheld!' He shifted his eyes looking pointedly in one direction. "But there is one of her sisters sitting down just behind you. She is very pretty, and I dare say very agreeable. You have made her acquaintance, so it is proper for you to ask her to dance."

Lifting his chin as if to place himself above the

revelers, Darcy looked about the room. "Which do you mean?" He caught Elizabeth's eye, and looked away. "You seem determined I should court Miss Elizabeth Bennet. She is tolerable, but there is nothing magical about her. And since no other men are seeking her out, I imagine I shall not waste my time with what other men slight."

He motioned toward Jane. "Your current love interest is smiling at you. Go enjoy her for you are wasting your time with me. See what you can learn from her—if you can keep your mind on our reason for being in this hamlet."

CHAPTER SIX
THE MYSTERY DEEPENS

Mr. Bingley left Darcy to his dark mood and joined Jane who stood near the refreshments. It was true Bingley fell in and out of love with a rapidity that irritated his friends, but this time was different. He could barely contain the warm rapture that flooded every part of his body when he saw Miss Jane Bennet. It was as if a giant halo engulfed them when they stood together.

Having heard Darcy's cutting remarks, Elizabeth hardened herself against the hurt. She joined Jane and Mr. Bingley, and by standing just outside their circle she was able to listen and observe how attentively the gentleman behaved toward her sister. He appeared to be smitten. Elizabeth would bide her time with them, knowing the opportunity to best that pompous pig, Darcy, would present itself soon enough.

Bingley handed Jane lemonade while forcing

himself to act on Darcy's instructions. "Please indulge my curiosity, for I have heard there are witches in Hertfordshire," he said while staring intently at Jane's lips as they touched the rim of the glass.

"I have always been intrigued with the legends of the London witches, and have heard there are different legends for the countryside," he said. "I have never met a true witch, and in a small community like Meryton, a person of magic might be more readily known."

Mr. Bingley's interest in witchcraft sparked an uneasy suspicion in Elizabeth. What motive could he have for inquiring about witches in Hertfordshire? Elizabeth fretted, as it was clear Jane had become enamored with the newcomer's warmhearted ways, and had relaxed her guard.

Aware that Darcy had drawn closer, Elizabeth thought to make light of Bingley's questions and turn the conversation away from witches by using mockery. "We do have a procedure in dealing with witches in our land of sheep paddies."

She skillfully aimed her sarcasm at Darcy's attitude of superiority. "Whenever we suspect someone of being a witch, we put them on one side of the butcher's scale, and a duck on the other. If the suspect weighs more than the duck, then we burn them—the duck that is—at the stake."

Jane giggled.

So intent were the men in their quest for a witch or a hermit, that it took them a moment to understand Elizabeth was joking. Bingley finally laughed, while Darcy raised one brow in contemplation of Miss Elizabeth Bennet's strange humor. Overcome with a sudden unexplainable need to impress her, he matched her wit with a touch of his own which was not far from the truth.

"In London," Darcy began, "when we find a witch we tie their fingers to their toes and throw them in the Thames. If they float they are witches. We fetch them from the water and dry them off so they do not smoke while we burn them at the stake."

Elizabeth could not resist returning Darcy's tease. "I fear you have not addressed the real issue: do witches weigh more than ducks?" She was oddly pleased to see two dimples appear in Darcy's cheeks even though he did not continue the repartee.

"I would be very disappointed to discover there really were no witches in Hertfordshire." Bingley exchanged meaningful looks with Darcy. "I would so enjoy meeting a real witch, but failing that, do you have any hermits?"

Elizabeth wondered if Mr. Bingley mistakenly took Hertfordshire for a mystic shop where one could obtain a witch, a goblin, or a hermit. A chill jigged down her spine. Why were they asking about hermits? Did they know about Herman the Hermit? Why would these Londoners be looking for a hermit? She feared they might be bounty hunters.

Lydia elbowed her way into their group; her face flushed from dancing. A young militiaman stood two steps behind her unable to break free from his enchantment with the youngest Bennet sister. Without waiting to be acknowledged, Lydia interrupted. "I overheard your query. We do have some very amusing witches in Hertfordshire!" she said. "I am sure you shall have no trouble making their acquaintance!"

Standing closer to Lydia, Elizabeth deliberately stepped on her sister's slippered toes.

"Ouch! You clumsy thing!" Lydia snapped, not taking the toe-tapping hint that she should govern her mouth. "As I was saying before *someone* stepped on my foot," she continued, "the cutest witch you will ever meet lives in Broom Cottage in Longbourn Woods. Her name is Fiona Feelgood." Lydia held her hand out chest-high. "Fiona is no taller than this and round as a puppy. She's a love witch."

"A love witch?" Darcy said with great interest.

Elizabeth saw a meaningful nod pass between the

two men. She knew she must nip this conversation before beans were spilled. "Lydia, please stop teasing Mr. Bingley and Mr. Darcy as it appears they are taking you seriously. Is that not Mr. Wickham I see just now entering the hall?" She looked toward the door.

Lydia's eyes lit up at the sight of George Wickham in his red militia uniform. She brushed her escort aside without uttering so much as an *excuse me.* With her ribbons flowing from her dark hair like flags from a ship at sea, she dashed to Wickham's side.

Darcy's face took on the look of a storm cloud. "George Wickham is not the best of companions for your sister. You might want to reclaim her."

The thought occurred to Elizabeth that Darcy was attempting to send her on a fool's errand to be rid of her, since he found her so unmagical. She had only just met Mr. Wickham and did not know much about him. Lydia was quite smitten with the handsome officer, but then any man in uniform would take her fancy.

CHAPTER SEVEN
CAROLINE BINGLEY

Caroline Bingley sashayed toward Darcy and Bingley. "May I join your little group?" She inserted herself next to Darcy. "What pray tell has you all so enthused?" She glanced around the room. "Is there someone worthy of juicy gossip on the dance floor?"

When no one responded, Miss Bingley addressed herself to Jane. "If Mr. Darcy or my brother have not told you yet, you are the loveliest woman in the room." She waited for a counter-compliment, or at least a protest from the gentlemen in which they named her as equal to Jane, but none came. Peeved, she turned to greet the arrival of her sister, Mrs. Hurst, who approached them as if she were afraid of being left out of a good chinwag.

Together, the two sisters began a stream of prattle detailing all of Jane's finer points, and managing to embarrass the poor girl. Their praise rang false to

Elizabeth as it was too much given too soon—they had not had the pleasure of her acquaintance for more than one evening.

The last dance was announced. A handsome young gentleman with ginger hair presented himself to Jane. She smiled politely, extended her hand and he walked her to the center of the room. The expression on Bingley's face was that of a dog who had lost his favorite bone.

Caroline Bingley held her breath, batting her eyes and gazing up at Mr. Darcy. But as they had already danced one dance, he would not commit to a second. She turned to watch the dancers, pretending to ignore his rejection.

Jane danced toward them, her pale blue gown swirling at her ankles, her blue ribbons flowing in her long blonde hair. At the moment she glided passed them, a large gray owl's feather fell from her hair and landed on the floor. The plume caught the attention of both Caroline and Elizabeth.

The plume, not pretty enough to be a lady's hair ornament, incited Caroline to snoopiness. She moved as if to avoid the dancers, then suddenly turned and dove between their feet to retrieve the feather.

Elizabeth launched herself in the direction of the fallen feather and beat Caroline to it by a smidge.

Sweeping the feather into her hand, Elizabeth tucked it into her décolletage, allowing herself a smug smile. The feather was a love message to Jane.

The Bingley sisters were up to no good, of that Elizabeth was now positive. Caroline and Mrs. Hurst were treating Jane nicely, perhaps to amuse themselves, but Elizabeth sensed there was another motive. She suspected their thoughts were dark, not evil-dark, but nasty-dark, which sometimes can be much worse than evil.

Too soon the ball was over. Bingley wished to reach out and touch Jane, but he dare not be so forward. And so he sent her tokens of his affection via longing glances with promises of things to come. "The ball cannot be over already. It is yet an hour before midnight. We must bring the gaiety of the ton to Meryton. I shall give a ball at Netherfield—soon. And we shall dance on until well after midnight." He beamed a warm smile at Jane.

Elizabeth felt eyes cutting in her direction and turned in time to catch Mr. Darcy staring an inscrutable stare. Perhaps the rogue sought some final way to best her before they parted. She graced him with a smile so impertinent it compelled him to look away.

The Bennet family exited the Meryton Assembly

Hall. As they waited their turn to enter the family carriage, Jane tapped her sister on the shoulder. "I have grown quite fond of Mr. Bingley," she said, softly.

Elizabeth had only to look in her sister's sparkling blue eyes to know that Jane had fallen in love much too quickly. This could not bode well as the moon was full. Elizabeth shivered.

CHAPTER EIGHT
THINGS THAT GO BUMP IN THE NIGHT

Bingley's carriage arrived at Netherfield without incident. The coachman helped Mrs. Hurst and then Caroline Bingley to alight. The night air was chilly but the ladies were well wrapped, and although Mrs. Hurst hurried to the door, Caroline moved slowly anticipating Darcy's movements and circling around him, much like a sheep dog shepherding a stray.

"See your family to bed and then meet me in the library," Darcy whispered to Bingley. "I will be in when I complete my odious task." He pulled a small empty crystal-clear bottle from his pocket and disappeared into the garden.

"Wait for me! You walk too quickly!" Caroline said, dashing to Darcy's side. "Is it not a lovely night for a stroll? She attempted to slip her arm in his, but he dodged her clutches while hiding the bottle in the palm of his hand. Does the full moon not set a romantic glow upon my gown?"

Darcy clenched his teeth to refrain from bellowing at the insufferable woman. "Miss Bingley, I wish to be alone. Please do not cause me to be rude."

"Are you not well?" she persisted.

The woman is as dense as a London fog. "I wish to meditate and to do so alone. You appear weary from the ball. Perhaps you need beauty sleep?"

Caroline touched her hand to her cheek, wondering if she *did* look tired. Suddenly panicked, she turned on her heels, dashed from the garden, and galloped up the staircase to her bedroom. Rousing her maid, she immediately removed her makeup and directed the woman to smear her face, neck, and arms with French beauty cream. And then for fear of smudging the ointment or developing sleeping creases on her face, she climbed into bed and positioned her head on four pillows, and struggled to fall asleep.

Meantime back in the garden, Darcy set about his task uncorking the small empty bottle and stepping cautiously into the freshly laid flowerbed. He soon accomplished his mission and lingered outside in the waning moonlight to allow enough time for Caroline Bingley to have removed herself for the evening.

Slipping the bottle inside his coat pocket, he stepped into the library, where he accepted a snifter of brandy from Bingley. "Your sister accosted me in the garden and would only leave when I became firm with her. We need to establish some rules or I will not be able to control my temper around her. If you have no objections, I shall require the use of this room in *complete* privacy if I am to get us out of this conundrum."

"Us? Please forgo the use of the terms *us and we*. This is something you have brought upon yourself. You must admit your ego is your worst enemy," Bingley said, "I was no party to what occurred in London."

He finished his brandy and returned the snifter to the silver tray on the desk. "Take this room for your secret use, but leave me the parlor for entertaining; I have plans," Bingley said.

Darcy held his snifter up to the candlelight, studying the shades of brown and gold that spun from the liquid. "You have plans again? You have given away chunks of your heart so many times, I doubt there is a morsel left."

"Allow me some happiness. I believe I am about to fall in real love."

"We are not here to make friends *or* lose our hearts. Concentrate on our mission or I shall have to adjust your thinking. And since you insist on keeping

Caroline here, kindly rein her in for she is constantly at my elbow. Should she discover my faux pas, she could use it for leverage over me."

"I will do my best, but you know she is determined to be your wife."

Darcy cringed. "That is exactly what I mean. She could blackmail me into marriage and I would be forced to defend myself for I shall never consent to marry your sister."

Bingley chose his words with care as Darcy was his dearest friend, but could be a powerful adversary. "I agree that Caroline is devious, manipulative, and completely without any redeeming value, but you cannot harm her—what did you have in mind?"

Darcy smiled; the tension lifted from between the two friends, as it once again became clear Bingley shared his irritation with Caroline. "I have not formulated a defense against her, but it would not be too painful." He poured himself another snifter of brandy and quaffed it down. "We must find the hermit called Herman before both our heads are placed on the chopping block in London. Do you think the love witch would know where to find him?"

"Fiona Feelgood?" Bingley asked.

"That is the only witch lead we have; I believe we must seek her assistance. Did Lydia Bennet not say the witch could be found at Broom Cottage in Longbourn Woods?" Darcy said. "We shall strike out for Miss Feelgood in the morning, but for now, leave me to my work. I will meet you at the stables after you have had your morning coffee."

Bingley left the library and Darcy locked the door behind his friend. He then tended to the small box. He finished his ministrations, and then fearing Caroline's snooping, he decided to take the treasure to his room for the night.

CHAPTER NINE
THE WITCH HUNT

Darcy sprang from his bed as a weak ray of sunlight slipped between the drapes. Gently he lifted the box from the bedside table and examined the contents. *Safe and sound.* They would seek out this Fiona Feelgood, and if she really were a witch, she would know where they could find the hermit who possessed the gift for undoing spells.

Dressing quickly, Darcy gently placed the box in his coat pocket and gingerly made his way from his bedchamber to the front door.

Half asleep in her room and with hours of sleep-time still before her, Caroline Bingley felt something tickle her face. She brushed the annoyance away with her hand. It prickled and refused to budge. Caroline swiped it again, but it did not move. Slowly opening her eyes, she ran her fingers over the shaft of a feather! It was growing from her chin! Her screams echoed through the halls of Netherfield.

As Darcy touched the handle on the front door, Caroline's bawl reached his ears. Since her morning cries were fairly routine; he slipped out the door and made for the stable to wait for Bingley.

Caroline dashed to the dressing table mirror. Her hands shook as she plucked the feather from her chin with a stinging yank. She held it up to the morning light. Though smaller in size than the feather that fell from Jane Bennet as she danced, it was a match in color. She decided then and there that she must ask Miss Bennet to dinner, today. She would invite her to come alone, as that sister of hers was a bit too keen.

Caroline tottered to the breakfast table and fell into a chair, exhausted from sleeping upright, and only now slightly recovered from discovering an owl feather growing from her chin.

Bingley stood at the sideboard filling his plate with ham, eggs, and a thin slice of pheasant, and then he took his place at the table. Clearing his throat, he took a soothing sip of tea. He felt a bit out of sorts and hoped he was not coming down with something, not with love so close at hand. Ignoring Caroline's melodramatic condition he spoke, "I have definitely decided to throw a ball at Netherfield. You will enjoy acting as hostess, won't you, sister? I imagine it would be best done before the Hursts return to London so they may attend. Will that allow you enough time to prepare?"

She stared at her brother with droopy eyes and did not respond.

"This morning's scream—was it anything out of the ordinary?" he asked less out of true concern and more as a courtesy.

"Nothing which I cannot control," she snarled. After confirming that both Darcy and Bingley would be away for the entire day, she determined to invite Jane Bennet to dinner. But first she set her mind to the little details that would make her brother's ball the event of the Hertfordshire season.

Bingley left his sister twittering over her plans for his event; unaware of the mischief she planned for the day. He set about to join Darcy in his hunt for the love witch and the hermit.

Once Caroline was alone at the breakfast table her mind wandered from Bingley's ball to how best to word an invitation which Jane Bennet could not refuse. She would get to the bottom of this feather bumblebroth, for it was most peculiar and smacked of witchcraft. The dark arts were not something Caroline would ever tolerate.

She toyed with the remains of her bread and butter

while her mind wandered to Fitzwilliam Darcy. Under ordinary circumstances his behavior was difficult, but over the past few days the change in his temperament left her rather curious.

If she could convince Darcy that she was on his side and would help him, then perhaps he might see the value in marrying her. If not, well then, there was always the fine art of blackmail. It had never been far from her mind as a last resort in securing his affections. But first she must catch the man while he was up to something worthy of blackmail.

She went to her writing desk and penned an invitation to Miss Jane Bennet.

CHAPTER TEN
THE INVITATION

Thomas Bennet repeated aloud his most frequent thought, "I think our two youngest daughters uncommonly foolish."

"My dear Mr. Bennet, you must not expect our girls to have the sense of their father and mother. When they get to our age, I dare say they will not think about militia officers any more than I do. At one time I fancied a red coat, and still find them to be handsome to look at. But if a smart young colonel with five or six thousand a year should want one of my girls I shall not say nay to him," she said.

Fanny Bennet swallowed a grin before she summed up the words to go with an image that trotted through her mind. "I thought Colonel Forster looked very becoming in his uniform the other night."

She was prevented from continuing her ramble when a footman entered the parlor with a note for Miss

Jane Bennet; it came from Netherfield. He waited for an answer.

Mrs. Bennet's heart began to race as she watched Jane open the letter; at last she was to meet with success. The scent of a wedding was in the wind. A sigh escaped her buxom chest as she thought, *one down and four to go.*

She could not contain herself and called out to Jane, "Who is it from? What is it about? Please make haste and tell us! I cannot bear the suspense."

Jane appeared bemused and yet pleased. "It is from *Miss* Bingley," she said and then read it aloud.

> *My dear friend*
>
> *If you are not so compassionate as to dine today with Louisa and me, we shall be in danger of hating each other for the rest of our lives. A whole day spent with one's sister and no other companion can never end without a quarrel. Come as soon as you can as my brother and Mr. Darcy are out for the day.*
>
> *—Yours ever, Caroline Bingley*

"Mr. Bingley will not be there," said Mrs. Bennet. "How unfortunate." She would have to plan around this obstacle.

Jane dispatched the Netherfield footman with her acceptance.

"Can I have the carriage?" she asked, taking for granted that she would have access to the family coach for an important social visit.

"No, my dear, you had better go on horseback, because it seems likely to rain and then you must stay all night. Won't that be grand?"

Hearing her mother's shameless scheme, Elizabeth clenched her hands in her lap, as she willed her steel embroidery needle to bend itself into a perfect U-shape, rendering it useless. But despite the needle bending, her temper continued to boil. That her mother would send her sister to Netherfield on horseback with a storm pending was something she could barely countenance.

"I would much prefer the coach," Jane said.

Mrs. Bennet wore her stubborn face. Elizabeth knew there would be no getting her to budge on the subject, for she could sense a husband drawing close. "Jane, dear, your father cannot spare the horses, I am sure. They are needed here. Mr. Bennet, are the horses not needed here?"

Elizabeth looked at her father hoping to catch his eye, for he did not refuse her—not that often.

Without looking up, and thereby avoiding

confrontation with his wife, he responded. "The horses are needed on the farm."

And so the die was cast. Jane would ride a horse in foul weather.

Elizabeth joined Jane in their shared bedroom as she changed to a proper dress and matching boots for her gallop to Netherfield. She helped her sister arrange her hair to withstand the jostling that was sure to occur as she trotted to dinner with Caroline Bingley and her sister, Mrs. Louisa Hurst.

"Do be careful Jane," she said, wondering if her sister had any premonitions about this jaunt. Jane had a way of knowing things before they happened. It was a gift she had inherited from their grandmother on their mother's side. Both Elizabeth and Jane were quite sure it was Grandma's magic that had enticed their father into proposing to their mother.

Before Elizabeth could question her sister, there came a flapping at the opened window and a large gray owl stepped from the ledge onto the inside sill, wrapping his long talons around the edge of the shelf.

Jane ran and knelt on the window seat, reached out her hand and stroked the bird's wide broad head. "Tristan, I know you do not approve, but Mother is adamant that I ride to Netherfield. And by the way, I appreciate the love-feathers but please do not send them to me when I am otherwise engaged. We do not wish to call attention to ourselves."

The owl turned his head slowly, moving his huge golden eyes from Jane to Elizabeth.

"It is beyond my control," Elizabeth told the owl. "Mother will have it no other way. And you shan't be able to accompany Jane. for you will attract attention and there will be assumptions."

At that moment, a sleek Siamese cat sauntered into the room and jumped into Elizabeth's arms. "Pyewacket. Where have you been?"

The cat let out a series of mews sounding almost like proper English sentences.

"Jane *must* go," Elizabeth said to her cat. "Mother insists. Do you have intuitions on the outcome of this adventure?"

The cat dropped from her arms and circled to the bedroom door and back, three times.

"Three passes," Elizabeth said with some level of comfort. "Pyewacket has given you his blessing. But I am still concerned about Mr. Bingley's and Mr. Darcy's interest in witches. Do be careful Jane. If ever there were witch hunters about those two men would fit the description."

Jane planted a light kiss on the top of her owl's feathery head, and looked out the window watching the storm clouds gather. "Well, if Pyewacket thinks the journey is worth enduring the storm, then I shall go. And no, I do not have any premonitions; I knew you were going to ask. I do find Mr. Bingley most appealing and that is clouding my visions."

"Just beware of Mr. Darcy, for I feel his energies are not under his control. There is something amiss with that man."

"You find him intriguing. You cannot fool me," Jane said, tweaking her sister on the tip of her turned up nose. "You be careful, lest you lose your steely heart."

Together the girls walked to the front door where Mrs. Bennet attended them, with many cheerful hopes for bad weather. Jane mounted the huge mare, and set out on the road to Netherfield as the sky darkened.

Mrs. Bennet stood waving to Jane. Elizabeth squinted her eyes at Mrs. Bennet's cap and it flew off the poor women's head; her hairpins began to pop free and fell to the floor with a tinkling sound.

"My heavens!" Mrs. Bennet yelped, placing her hands on her head and looking about as if to find the spirit who toyed with her hair. "I hate when that happens!"

Picking her cap from the floor, she scurried to her bedroom. Her weather hopes were soon answered for

Jane had not been gone long before it rained heavily. Elizabeth was concerned, but Mrs. Bennet was delighted.

CHAPTER ELEVEN
THE LOVE WITCH

Darcy and Bingley devoted most of the morning to slowly riding the boundaries of the Longbourn estate, seeking an opening into the dense forest that was Longbourn Woods. Broom Cottage could be hidden anywhere along the border. Witches, like hermits, preferred the darkest woods. And the two friends were being very cautious in leaving no shrubbery unexplored.

Just after noon, the rolling pastures finally came to a dead end in the northeast corner of the estate, running smack into thick spruce and boxwood trees. An overgrown footpath lay before them. "There is enough room if we ride single file," Darcy said.

"Right or left?" Bingley asked.

"Which way, Parsifal?" Darcy said.

The stallion turned to the right.

"Right it is."

They moved at a cautious pace, peering into the dark forest, looking for sight of Broom Cottage. Darcy reined in his horse and Bingley followed suit. They had come to a weathered sign in the road with an arrow pointing toward an overgrown path. It read, *Witchduck Lane.*

Darcy chuckled remembering the banter at the Meryton ball. "A witch and a duck, indeed, Miss Elizabeth," he whispered to himself.

The men followed the path to a tiny white cottage tucked under a willow tree. The little house appeared to be dropped in the middle of a riot of wild flowers. A white picket fence enclosed the thatched roof bungalow, and a sign on the gate read *Broom Cottage.*

Dismounting, they tied their horses to the fence and walked up the gray stone path. Would a love witch possess a wart-bearing hooknose and a high black hat? Darcy wondered.

Window boxes of brightly colored flowers sat under the lace-curtained mullion windows. The front steps bore twinkling stones embedded between the flat slabs of slate. A brass plate near the door read:

FIONA FEELGOOD ~ LOVE WITCH, LTD.

Darcy rapped on the weathered oak door using the heart-shaped brass knocker.

There was no response.

He knocked again, this time employing three rapid knocks. He shrugged at Bingley. "Perhaps the charm of three will work?"

"Coming!" A sweet little voice chirped.

A little dumpling of a woman of undefined age opened the door. She had the face of a freckled cherub and a towel wrapped around her head. "Sorry, I was washing my hair. Were you waiting long?"

Darcy choked on a laugh. This little round person was not the hooked nose, skin and bones shrew he had anticipated.

"Have you not seen a wet-headed witch before? If you are looking for a love spell, you had best treat me with respect," she cut him a playful look. "Now tell me what you desire before I invite you into my cottage."

"Are you Miss Fiona Feelgood? Can you remove spells?" Darcy asked.

"Yes and no. I am Fiona Feelgood. But I cannot remove spells. Are you witch hunters?"

"Do we look like witch hunters?" Darcy snapped, his patience running thin.

"Yes. In fact you both do, although your friend appears to be smitten. Is he?"

"He is," Darcy said, nodding at Bingley.

"I am in natural love and under no spell—that I know of," Bingley said.

Miss Fiona Feelgood's warm brown eyes twinkled merrily. "So how can I help you gentlemen?"

"We require the removal of a spell. We understand that a hermit by the name of Herman—"

Boom! Thunder cut the air.

Darcy and Bingley looked up at the sky. They were due for a soaking if they did not hurry along.

Fiona frowned and slammed the door in their faces.

Darcy knocked again. The second time he touched the knocker he received a shock as if a bolt of lightning awaited his touch. The little witch's voice could be heard through the door. "Do not mention that libertine's name again or I will make it storm for a fortnight!"

"What does witchcraft smell like?" Bingley asked, "Because I smell something damp and moldy." He backed away from the door.

Raising his voice theatrically, to be sure the little witch heard, Darcy called out as if addressing Bingley. "Perhaps I should offer a huge reward for an introduction to this hermit?"

The cottage door popped open and Miss Feelgood stuck out her toweled head. "I shall think about it." The door nipped closed just as quickly as it had opened.

"You can find us at Netherfield Park!" Darcy shouted.

Darcy and Bingley ran through the downpour to their horses, with the little witch calling from her front steps, "What kind of reward?" Her words were lost on the wind.

They mounted with buckets of cold English rain falling on their heads. Wordlessly, they galloped back to Netherfield. Upon their arrival Bingley was delighted to be told that Miss Jane Bennet was huddled in one of the guest bedchambers. Instantly distressed at her condition, but thrilled to have her so close, he knocked on the bedchamber door.

Jane pulled the coverlet to her chin as she responded to his knock. "Please do not come in, for it would be unseemly!" she said. She also knew that despite the assistance of Miss Bingley's maid, her appearance was not what she would have him see.

Mr. Bingley spoke through the door. "I would not think of entering your room. But promise me, should you require anything during the night, you will ring for my sister's maid."

"I promise," she said, her voice cracking.

The rain continued the entire evening.

Jane did not return to Longbourn.

Taking the credit for the rain as well as the unfortunate idea, Mrs. Bennet more than once bragged of sending her daughter out into the storm.

That was until the next morning when a servant from Netherfield brought the following note for Elizabeth:

My Dearest Lizzy,

I find myself very unwell this morning, which I suppose is because I was wet through and through yesterday. My kind friends will not hear of my returning till I am better. They have insisted on my seeing Mr. Jones, the apothecary, therefore do not be alarmed if you should hear of his having been to me. I have a sore throat and a headache, but there is not much else the matter with me.

Your loving sister,

J.

Elizabeth finished reading the note aloud and could not help but glare at her mother.

"Well, my dear," said Mr. Bennet to his wife, "if your daughter should have a dangerous fit of illness, if she should die, it should be comfort to you to know that it was all in pursuit of Mr. Bingley, and under your orders."

Mrs. Bennet, a transparent person, wore a defensive expression as she countered his sarcasm by saying, "Oh, I am not afraid of Jane's dying. People do not die of little colds. She will be taken good care of. As long as she stays there, it is all very well. Now if I could have the carriage, I would go see her."

"But you know the carriage is not to be had!" Mr. Bennet snapped, both stressed from his wife's schemes and worried about Jane's health.

Elizabeth did not have a good feeling about her sister's condition. "I am going to Jane," she announced. She was no horsewoman, and without the carriage, walking was her only alternative.

"Do not be silly," cried her mother, "it rained last night. If you walk in all that mud you will not be fit to be seen when you get there."

"I shall be fit enough to see my sister, which is all I want!"

"Lizzy, should I send for the horses and have the carriage arranged?" Mr. Bennet had woken to the situation and wished to aid Elizabeth in tending to her sister.

"No. I want to walk. It is only three miles, which is nothing when one has a motive. I shall be back by dinner."

CHAPTER TWELVE
SIX INCHES OF MUD

Elizabeth went up to her bedroom, gathered some paper wrapped herbs from her drawer, and placed them carefully in her reticule. Collecting her cloak and her walking boots she headed for Netherfield accompanied on her hike by Pyewacket at her heels and Tristan flying from tree to tree above her.

Dashing through the fields at a quick pace, she jumped over stiles and climbed over fences. She sprung over puddles with impatience, as Pyewacket walked along the grassy shoulder of the road. After a long messy trek Elizabeth at last found herself within view of Netherfield. Her legs were weary and her stockings dirty, but her face glowed with the warmth of exercise.

As Elizabeth climbed the long, formal staircase, Pyewacket darted into the flowerbed near the front entrance to wait, and Tristan perched on the second floor window ledge. Not caring a smidge for her appearance, she lifted the silver knocker and waited impatiently for, she had come so far and could delay no longer in seeing to her sister's health.

After what seemed a very long time, but was in fact only a few minutes, an elderly butler answered her knock. Once Elizabeth introduced herself and explained her mission she was shown into the breakfast-parlor, where all except Jane were at their meal.

Clearly startled to see her, Mr. Bingley jumped from his seat. Caroline remained in her chair and studied Elizabeth through beady eyes. That Miss Bennet should walk three miles so early in the day, in such muddy weather, and by herself, was both shocking and curious to Miss Bingley and Mrs. Hurst. Their contempt for her walk and her condition became evident, although on the surface, they received her politely.

Mr. Bingley conveyed only good humor and kindness, Mr. Darcy said very little, and Mr. Hurst nothing at all. The former was intrigued by the vibrancy the exercise had given to her complexion, while doubting her sister was sick enough for Elizabeth to take such a risk. The latter gentleman was thinking of nothing more than his breakfast.

Ignoring their stares, she immediately asked after

her sister, but the news was not favorable. Miss Bennet had not slept well, and though awake, she was feverish, not strong enough to leave her room. Mr. Bingley suggested he would escort Elizabeth to Jane's room, and excused himself from the table.

As Elizabeth stepped back to await Mr. Bingley, she caught sight of Caroline Bingley wrinkling her nose at the mud-covered edge of Elizabeth's petticoat. She was only vaguely aware that filth clung to the hem of her underdress in a thick brown layer.

Hand to mouth, Miss Bingley leaned toward Mr. Darcy to call his attention to it. Her voice carried, "See that? There is at least six inches of mud attached to the bottom of her skirt."

But before Darcy could look, Elizabeth willed the mud to disappear. Caroline looked back and the mud was gone. Darcy's brows knit in a frown as he thought for the thousandth time since first meeting his friend's sister: *what was the hen-witted woman talking about?* "Enough, Miss Bingley. Your imagination tries my patience."

Bingley, with great care, walked Elizabeth upstairs to the room where her sister rested. Not wishing to cause Jane any discomfort, he did not follow Elizabeth into the room, but rather spoke to Jane from the half-opened doorway, "Should you need anything, please do not hesitate to ask me, or any member of my household. I am so sorry you are ill."

Jane appeared tiny and faded in the huge four-poster bed. She extended her hand and reached for Elizabeth, delighted to see her. She had not wished to alarm anyone in Netherfield, or her family, but she felt a desperate need for comforting.

She seemed quite weak and Elizabeth did not prod her for conversation, although she repeated her thankfulness for the kindnesses she had received from the Bingley family. But then Jane was always generous with her compliments.

Elizabeth allowed the ever-protective Tristan to enter via the window for just long enough to relieve his owl mind, and then for his own protection, she shooed him away and closed the window. Knowing they would not be alone for too long, she refrained from unwrapping her herbs for fear the potent smells might be questioned.

When breakfast was over, Jane and Elizabeth were joined by Bingley' sisters. They soon won Elizabeth over with the affection and solicitude they showed Jane. Mr. Jones, the apothecary, came and examined his patient. He agreed with the general consensus, that she had caught a violent cold and they must bring it under control.

He advised her to stay in bed at least one more day and to drink some draughts he provided. Elizabeth quickly administered the medicines, and settled Jane back under the downy coverlet.

Poor Jane's head ached acutely. She slept on and off while her sister sat at her bedside. When the clock struck three, Elizabeth felt she must return home and very unwillingly said so.

Caroline Bingley offered the use of their carriage to Elizabeth, but when Jane heard of her sister's parting she was very upset. Seeing her distress, Miss Bingley changed her offer, inviting Elizabeth to stay the night. Both Bennet sisters were most grateful to Miss Bingley. A servant was sent to Longbourn to inform the family and to bring back clothing and a few personal items.

Darcy paced the parlor, unable to concentrate as they had yet to find the hermit who might be able to undo the wrongful spell. What made him think he could follow in his mother's footsteps? She was a much respected practitioner of the light art of magic. Twenty generations back, Lady Anne Darcy's ancestor had used white witchcraft to save England from invasion by the Vikings.

It was vanity that led Darcy to think, to agree to—reluctantly—cast a spell that was to help England, but now might mean his downfall and also that of the

British monarchy. And to complicate the stew in a delicious but unacceptable way, he felt an odd attraction to Miss Elizabeth Bennet—despite the difference in their status. Once he had learned of his mother's skills in witchcraft, he felt himself set above mere mortals. There was no one he could ever trust with his secret except Bingley.

Besides the lack of any intelligent, discreet ladies in London, Darcy had always felt he carried this dark secret that could not be shared through marriage, as it would put a burden on his wife and children. Gossip was the religion of the ladies of London. Darcy kept his own counsel, as he knew that a secret is not a secret if more than one person knows it—except for Bingley. He trusted his friend with his life.

The power he had inherited put him at risk, both of losing his fortune and his life. A wife like Caroline Bingley, with her mindless yammering, could be the death of him. If ever there were an heir to the Darcy family estate in Derbyshire, then it would be up to his younger sister Georgiana produce the successor.

CHAPTER THIRTEEN
DINNER AND INSULTS

At half-past six Elizabeth was summoned to dinner. Everyone inquired as to Jane's condition, but only Bingley seemed sincerely interested. The plain fact of the matter was that Jane was no better.

The Bingley sisters, on hearing of Jane's lack of progress, repeated three or four times how much they were concerned for her and how dreadful it was to have a bad cold. Then, thinking no more of Jane, they waffled on about how they disliked being ill themselves and set about describing their battles with poor health. Their self-centered blathering caused Elizabeth to readjust her thinking about them. They had quickly slipped into a decline in her esteem.

Their brother was the only one of the group who seemed to share her anxiety for Jane. His attention to her sister's unfortunate condition and his kindnesses to Elizabeth prevented her from feeling so much an intruder as she believed the others considered her.

Miss Bingley was busily immersed in Mr. Darcy and her sister, Louisa, was merely tolerant of Elizabeth presence. Mr. Hurst was a cypher, he lived only to eat, drink, and play cards. And Mr. Darcy watched Elizabeth with what she could only guess was suspicion.

During dinner, Mr. Bingley addressed Elizabeth. "Miss Bennet, I understand you enjoy reading. Please feel free to avail yourself of my library. It is embarrassingly sparse of quality books as I am not a reader, but I hope to improve that once I am settled in Netherfield."

"Thank you, Mr. Bingley. That is kind of you. I may accept your offer as there is nothing like a good book to help one pass the time," she said.

When dinner was over Elizabeth returned directly to Jane's bedside. No sooner had she left the room then Caroline Bingley began to lay insults upon her. She found Elizabeth manners impertinent; she had no conversation, no style, and no beauty. She rattled on, designing her words to alter any good feelings Darcy might be developing toward Elizabeth.

Louisa Hurst joined her sister, declaring that Elizabeth had nothing to recommend her but being an excellent walker. "I shall never forget her appearance this morning. She looked almost wild. She is so…so…rustic!"

Caroline arched her neck lifting her head high as she delivered yet another insult designed to turn Mr. Darcy against Elizabeth.

"She did, indeed, Louisa. I could hardly keep from laughing. How preposterous is the very idea of scampering about the countryside because her sister has a cold? Did you see her hair? How untidy! How blowsy!"

Louisa Hurst nodded in agreement, while Mr. Bingley's face turned into a tight frown.

Once begun, Caroline Bingley could not stop her barrage. "And her petticoat. I hope you saw it, six inches deep in mud, I am absolutely certain. And the dress which she let down to cover it did not help at all."

"This was all lost upon me," Mr. Bingley said. "I thought Miss Elizabeth Bennet looked remarkably well when she came into the room this morning. Her dirty petticoat quite escaped my notice."

"You did not see it, and Mr. Darcy did not see it," she said. "Well, I *tell you* it was dirty! Why will no one believe me?" She felt a tickle at the corner of her lips. Raising her serviette to cover her mouth, she found a feather stuck between her teeth. Shaken but determined to hide the beastly thing, Miss Bingley plucked it from her jaw, tucked it in the cloth and placed it in her lap. Something must be done with the woman, for strange things were happening since their arrival in Netherfield and she wished to place the blame at Elizabeth's muddy feet.

Darcy pinned Caroline with his eyes. "I find a literate woman—with or without a dirty petticoat—to be a pleasant change. I imagine when her mind is not dwelling on her sister's health Miss Elizabeth Bennet is capable of providing interesting conversation, for I gather she is well read."

Caroline's eyes were hooded as she shot angry looks at her brother. Her brother had forbidden her to enter the library to allow Darcy privacy, but now Elizabeth Bennet was warmly invited! She gazed at the man she so fancied. Darcy caught her looking and turned away in disgust.

Not one to drop a topic while there was still some life in it, Caroline said, "I *know* I saw the mud on her petticoat, and then poof! It disappeared!" Another feather shot from her lips when she poofed, but since no one noticed, she continued her harangue. "Jane Bennet shared this little tidbit with me. They have relatives in the *Wapping* section of London! You know the area of which I speak; it is where witches once dwelt until they were driven away. Does that not sound suspicious?"

As no one commented, she gave it one more poke. "I swear I have seen Elizabeth Bennet's eyes turn red!"

Darcy excused himself from the table without addressing Caroline's accusations.

***

Elizabeth found it impossible to sleep as she sat on the loveseat in Jane's room. It was as if the seat were stuffed with rocks. She adjusted her slippered feet on the ottoman and gathered her robe around her. Thankfully, the Netherfield footman had returned promptly with clothing for both herself and Jane. Eliz shuddered at the thought of borrowing a nightdress and dressing gown from Miss Bingley as the woman would be sure to call attention to how she towered over Elizabeth with her elegant form.

A wicked little thought entered Elizabeth's mind; she could borrow one of Mr. Darcy's shirts as a sleeping gown as it would surely cover her to her ankles. She smiled and cast the image aside. *Where did that idea come from?*

The tension of being unable to sleep and the worry over Jane thrust Elizabeth into such a state as only a good book might relieve. Mr. Bingley had offered her access to his library, and although the look on Mr. Darcy's face was off-putting, she would not be put off, for when Elizabeth Bennet needed a book, she needed a book! She glanced at the mantle clock. It was well after the witching hour.

Elizabeth eased from the bedroom, careful not to awaken Jane. Tiptoeing down the hall, she dashed lightly down the carpeted staircase. The house was silent.

She eased open the library door, slipped inside, and softly closed it.

With a gasp, she slammed herself against the wall directly behind the closed door. Mr. Darcy stood at a huge oak desk that dominated the room; he was holding a small box. Even in the dim candlelight she could see it was a lovely green and gold enameled square. He looked up at the sound of her entrance, his expression fierce. They stood frozen, staring at each other.

Elizabeth was not one for loud confrontations and sought to ease the situation before Darcy raised his voice in anger. She was about to explain why she had come to the library, when the door opened and Bingley stepped into the room.

"Have you had any luck?" he began, ignorant of Elizabeth's presence. He jumped when he saw her standing behind the door. "Miss Bennet," he stammered. "Is your sister not well?"

"She is sleeping soundly, thank you for asking. I do wish to prevail on your kind offer of borrowing a book. I find reading helps me to relax, and at the moment I find myself rather tense with worry."

"That is very understandable. Please, choose any book," Bingley said. He stood nervously watching Darcy for a reaction, as the library was to be Darcy's private domain. The taller gentleman slipped the small green box into a desk drawer, closed it with a click, and waited impatiently for Elizabeth to make her choice.

Feeling Darcy's eyes upon her, she gave the shelves a quick glance, grabbed a small brown book without looking at the title, and thanked Mr. Bingley. She scurried out the door with a polite goodnight. Normally, Elizabeth would love to wander a library—any library. But Darcy's angry glare had made that impossible.

Dashing up the stairs to Jane's sleeping chamber, she closed the door behind her, and let a shiver run through her body. There was something seriously wrong at Netherfield.

CHAPTER FOURTEEN
NETHERFIELD – DAY TWO

Mrs. Bennet arrived just before breakfast. She pronounced Jane unfit for travel and allowed that if Mr. Bingley would be so kind, she would feel less concerned if her daughters were to remain at Netherfield for one more day.

Bingley was beside himself with joy, for the longer he felt the warm glow of Jane's presence within the walls of his home, the happier he was. Never having experienced such a state of contentment, his mood bordered on euphoric. If only his friend Darcy could experience similar joy.

Mrs. Bennet devoted the entire length of her stay, which seemed much longer than three hours, to glorifying the beauties of Hertfordshire, making it seem the ideal place for a man of Mr. Bingley's stature to reside. She reached her most insufferable apex before finding her way out the door. Everyone at Netherfield, including the staff, breathed a collective sigh of relief as her carriage disappeared down the road.

With Jane and Elizabeth continuing to stay on, Caroline Bingley held mixed emotions as she was pleased to continue the drama of caring for a sick friend, but at the same time she sensed the growing attraction of Darcy to Elizabeth. No one else would have noticed the flirtation, but she had made a career of studying the man and could read the light that shined in his eyes when he spoke of the brown-eyed hoyden.

Elizabeth accompanied Jane down to the parlor after their hosts had finished their dinner. She sensed Darcy's eyes upon her. Was he looking for reasons to find fault? Was he waiting for her to question him about the green box? Elizabeth wanted to inform him she would never pry, as it was not her way. But the truth was, she *would* pry—not outright, for outright prying was rude, but Elizabeth did find subversive prying to be a delightful way to pass the time.

Within an hour of listening to the endless chatter of Miss Bingley and Mrs. Hurst, Jane grew tired. Making their excuses, Elizabeth helped her sister back to their room.

Once Jane was tucked in bed for the night, Elizabeth found herself in an uncomfortable position, as she was wide-awake with nothing to read. The book she had chosen in haste the night before was embarrassingly inappropriate: *The Gentleman's Guide to the Care of Dueling Pistols*. A duel, other than verbal, was not something she anticipated. Restless and, if she admitted it, eager for a bit of banter, she wandered downstairs, and returned to the parlor.

Mr. Bingley, Louisa Hurst and her husband were playing cards and based on the comments at the table, it appeared to be a game of loo. Darcy sat at the writing desk swatting Miss Bingley aside like a pesky insect, as she buzzed around him pollinating him with compliments on everything from his posture to his penmanship. The woman was an abomination.

Elizabeth quietly took a seat, the dueling book tucked under her shawl, and a smirk upon her face as she listened to the repartee between Mr. Darcy and Miss Bingley. The woman could not be more dense if she were thickened with flour. She refused to take his rejection literally and made light of his harsh words as if he were teasing her.

Having endured all she could, but fearing she would burst into laughter at one more Darcy-borne insult bouncing off the redhead, Elizabeth took the opportunity to approach Mr. Bingley as he left the card table.

"Mr. Bingley, may I impose on the hospitality of your library one more time? I should like to find another book," she said.

Darcy overheard her. "You *do* read quickly, Miss Bennet. Did you not enjoy the book you chose last evening?" A dimple played at the corner of his mouth. He spoke as if he knew the exact tome she had chosen the night before.

"I did. It was most informative," she said, not allowing her expression to reveal her embarrassment.

"Well, do not let me detain you in your quest for another book. I admire a lady who reads."

"I read!" Miss Bingley chirped, but neither Darcy nor Elizabeth paid her any mind. They locked eyes and something feverish passed between them. Elizabeth failed to muffle the gasp that escaped her throat as her face flushed crimson.

"You chose to pass the evening reading rather than succumb to a need for socializing," Darcy said. "I can appreciate that for it is my pleasure as well."

"Oh, shocking!" cried Miss Bingley. "To hear Mr. Darcy admit to any pleasure! How shall we punish him for such a revelation? What pleasure shall we deny him?"

"Intimate as you are with Mr. Darcy, you must know how to un-pleasure him," Elizabeth said to Miss

Bingley. The remark flew passed her like an arrow but struck Mr. Darcy, and he chuckled.

Miss Bingley angered at his snigger. "I would not expose myself to his laughter. My intimacy with Mr. Darcy is of the most distant kind."

"And I would keep it that way," Darcy said, staring down his nose at Miss Bingley.

"I should say that no one likes to be the object of laughter. Certainly not me!"

Elizabeth smiled. "Oh but I dearly love to be laughed at. It is an uncommon thing, but when it does occur it gives me much felicity."

"Then we must find some fault in you to provide us with a laugh," Darcy said.

"Do not attempt to ridicule what is wise and good in me, for I will defend my qualities to the death," she said, flashing her dark eyes upon him. "My follies are numerous enough to provide entertainment even for myself, but my virtues are beyond reproach," she said arching her eyebrows. "I suppose you are without faults, Mr. Darcy?"

Feeling he could not let her challenge rest, he responded. "It has been the study of my life to avoid those weakness which often expose one to ridicule."

Elizabeth struggled to keep the grin from her face as she spoke. "Such as vanity and pride?"

Unable to resist Darcy responded, "Yes, vanity is a weakness indeed. But pride, where there is real superiority of mind or talents, pride is always acceptable."

"But if talents are inherited—a gift from our ancestors—then one has no right to be prideful," Elizabeth said.

Darcy appeared stunned. Did this woman know the secret of his inheritance?

Miss Bingley stood there, watching them exchange verbal swipes as if engaged in a game of lawn tennis. Her mind, not being as swift as theirs, prevented her from engaging in their banter.

Seeing the spark of attraction in Darcy's eyes, Elizabeth was overcome with a feeling of uneasiness. It would not do to allow feelings for this man, as he might very well be a dark soul—a witch hunter. Her grandmother had warned her of such beings.

"With Mr. Bingley's permission, I shall make a brief visit to the library and then return to my sister's bedside." She clutched her shawl around her, covering the dueling book from view.

At that moment the butler entered the room and spoke to Mr. Bingley. Elizabeth held her breath when she heard him say, "There is a rather diminutive but determined lady at the door. She insists on speaking to both Mr. Bingley and Mr. Darcy. She is unaccompanied."

"At this time of night? A lady without an escort? What name does she offer?" Bingley asked.

"Miss Fiona Feelgood," the butler said.

CHAPTER FIFTEEN
MISS FIONA FEELGOOD

Elizabeth covered her mouth with her hand to muffle her scream of dismay. Mr. Darcy and Mr. Bingley had found the love witch! What could they possibly want from her unless they were witch hunters?

Bingley motioned Darcy to his side. They exchanged whispers and after hasty apologies to the assemblage, they left the room.

A wave of agitation washed over Elizabeth and she gasped for air as she felt she might drown. Miss Fiona Feelgood could mean trouble for Jane and Elizabeth; for although the little lady possessed a sweet heart, she was given to fits of bragging, and with bragging came a loose lip. The more Elizabeth thought about it, the surer she was that Mr. Darcy and Mr. Bingley were witch hunters. Her instincts about people were rarely wrong.

Caroline had taken Bingley's place at the card table.

While the others were thoroughly involved in the game, Elizabeth slipped toward the parlor door and stood just inside the room at the doorway to the hall. She cleared her head of all thoughts and concentrated on hearing what was being said in the foyer.

Mr. Bingley spoke in his usual gracious manner. Although Darcy was silent, the tension of his presence cut the air.

"What is it that has brought you here alone at night? Have you suddenly recalled your knowledge of the hermit?" Bingley asked.

"Perhaps…" Miss Feelgood's voice was light like the crackle of paper held in a fist.

"Have you reconsidered our offer?" Darcy said.

"I *am* here about the reward. But it will be of my choosing," she said.

Not one to waste a moment, Darcy snapped at the little witch. "So you admit you know where Herman the Hermit can be found?"

"I do. But it will cost you," she said. "I wish to be compensated for the risk I will take in revealing the secrets of another witch."

"What do you want, woman?" Darcy snapped; his patience strung thin as a violin string.

"I seek something that was once owned by your mother, Lady Anne Darcy," she said. "Come to Broom

Cottage the morning after Mr. Bingley's ball and I will tell you. I shall be busy until then, as love witches work their magic during balls. And I have backorders for love spells that you would not believe."

Darcy stared into Miss Feelgood's eyes, and found he could read her desires. It was an uncomfortable talent, one that humiliated him as it was akin to seeing people unclothed. But he was determined to use all the gifts he possessed to undo the wrong he had done, even if that meant entering their most secret thoughts.

An image of Miss Feelgood holding a dried rose in her tiny hands came to his vision. If a dead flower was all this lady required, he would gladly provide it. He had heard that country witches were eccentric, but this was almost too easy.

"If it is in my power, you shall have your wish," Darcy said.

"Lovely!" Fiona Feelgood said. "It is nothing you need nor will you miss it.

Now toodle-loo! My cauldron bubbles over."

The men escorted Miss Feelgood to the door, promising to attend her at Broom Cottage the day after the Bingley Ball.

Elizabeth's worries closed in on her like a thick fog. *This is what comes from helping Limited Edition witches.* She lived in fear of Fiona's little pink lizard of a tongue betraying her secret.

What treasure did Fiona Feelgood require from Darcy and Bingley? Would the little witch reveal the location of the hermit? Sighing a deep, heavy sigh, she told herself there was nothing to be gained by worrying. She left her listening post and stepped quickly to the library.

With the dueling book slipped back in its spot on the shelf she perused the small collection of novels. Any book she took might be subject to ridicule by Mr. Darcy and so she chose an adventure novel, Daniel Defoe's *Robinson Crusoe,* although she had read it at least twice before.

Elizabeth snuggled in an oversized armchair to read the first few chapters by the warmth of the huge fireplace before returning to Jane's beside. Her mind drifted to Fiona Feelgood. Had she been wrong to help the love witch when her spell had gone astray? She could not undo the incantation, but she did the first thing that came to her mind. Perhaps it wasn't best idea she had ever had, and it still remained to be undone.

The coziness of the fireplace, the boredom of re-reading a book she'd read before, and the pure bone-tiredness of worrying about Jane, caused Elizabeth to nod off. She was deep in a dream where an unknown figure chased her round a lovely English garden, when she was awakened by the sound of two people arguing. By the high pitch of one voice, she knew it was Caroline Bingley and the deep baritone of the other informed her it was Mr. Darcy.

"Do not touch this desk. For that matter, do not enter this room!" Darcy's voice sounded like thunder.

"I will do as I please. Netherfield is my brother's house, and I shall be mistress of it," Caroline Bingley sassed. "Until he marries, and perhaps he never will."

"This may be your brother's home, but while I am using this room or any room as mine, you will respect my privacy!" Darcy barked.

Back and forth they argued, until with a stamp of her foot, Caroline Bingley stormed out of the room.

Hearing Caroline exit, Elizabeth peeked around the high-backed wing of the chair. Unaware of her presence, Darcy touched a spot on the desk and a drawer slid open. Elizabeth watched with great curiosity. Embarrassed to admit she was eavesdropping, Elizabeth remained hidden.

Darcy took out the same green box he had held yesterday, and peered inside. All was well. He put the lid on and carefully placed the box on a high shelf between two stacks of books. Then silent as a shadow, he exited the library via the French doors that led to the garden.

Once he was gone, Elizabeth inched toward the hall door, ready to make a mad dash up the staircase, but from the corner of her eye she noticed the box moving on the shelf. It appeared to be hopping toward the edge. If it fell, whatever it contained would surely break or... Elizabeth flew to catch it and it dropped into her hand with an odd *thump-clump!*

The box made a raspy noise as it vibrated in her hand. There were a series of holes in the top of the box, which fit snuggly on the base. Unable to resist, Elizabeth slowly pried the lid, prepared to drop the box and run if it contained a rat or something equally as vile.

CHAPTER SIXTEEN
THE BOX

The lid came off with a snap. A shinny green frog sat in the box and looked up at Elizabeth. His soft brown eyes were filled with tears. She stroked his head and he seemed comforted by her touch. Why did Darcy keep a frog in a box? If he was a witch hunter, perhaps this was a witch? "Who are you?" she asked the frog. It held itself more erect but did not respond.

Fearing she would appear to be a snoop of the Caroline Bingley subspecies, and despite feeling sorry for the frog, Elizabeth replaced the lid. She could feel the little fellow thump about inside the container, but she knew she must return the box to the shelf or risk discovery.

Standing on tiptoe she was unable to reach the shelf. There was an easier way to right the box, but she had promised herself she would not use magic ever again, not unless a dire emergency presented itself. The accident with Herman the Hermit still hung guilty over her conscience. Magic came in handy but it also came with consequences.

She looked about the room for something to stand upon. The desk chair was much too large to move, she thought to make a pile of books, but that would be too time consuming. What if Darcy returned? He would think her the biggest snoop in the world—next to Caroline Bingley.

It was then she noticed a library ladder leaning against the far fall. Placing the frog box on the desk, she rolled the ladder along the wooden floor until it was properly situated just below the shelf.

Holding the box in her left hand, and gripping the ladder rail with a sweaty right hand, she carefully took two steps up and was just placing her foot on the third rung when Darcy entered through the French doors, his mouth dropped open at the sight of her on the ladder. *Caught in the act!*

He dashed toward her controlling the urge to yell out for fear of frightening her, but it was too late.

Elizabeth was so startled by his presence that she let out a squeak. Loosing her one-handed grip on the ladder but clinging to the frog box with her other hand, she tumbled into Darcy's arms. He caught her, but dropping the small cup of water and the glass bottle he carried.

It all happened so quickly, Darcy did not know whether to growl or laugh. In his attempt to catch Elizabeth and save the falling cup of water and the bottle, he lost his balance and fell to the floor. Elizabeth landed on top of him. They lay nose to nose, each caught up in something larger than a mere tumble.

They lay there, Elizabeth on top of Darcy, neither one wishing to admit this was reality. *Perhaps if I close my eyes I will wake from this silly dream*, she thought. Although she closed her eyes, it did nothing to change the simple fact that she lay on top of Fitzwilliam Darcy, pompous toff and possible witch hunter. Elizabeth could not help but sink into Darcy's deep soulful eyes. Inhaling, she smelled his breath, savoring the scent of fresh air and brandy. He *was* a yummy gentleman, but now it was time to get off.

She released her grip on the frog box and placed it gently on the floor near their shoulders, hoping the little creature was not injured in her fall. The expression on Darcy's face was inscrutable. Would he forever regard her as a snoop?

Just as she began to remove herself from his warm, hard body, the lid came off the box and the frog hopped out. He skipped over to their faces and stared from one to the other, as they lay almost cheek-to-cheek.

Meow!

They turned their heads at the sound of a cry that came from near the garden doors. A slender black cat studied them with what could only be deemed a cat-sarcastic glance. He sashayed toward them placing one paw in front of the other as if walking on a tightrope.

The feline had yet to notice the little green creature that sat on the far side of Darcy and Elizabeth's heads. Cats are better equipped to see their prey when it is in motion. The frog stood still, frozen with fear.

Ribbit! The frog croaked, unable to contain its terror.

The cat, now alerted to the frog, crouched low, ready to spring. The frog wiggled between Darcy and Elizabeth's chests. It all happened so quickly that any decorum was lost in the chaos that broke out.

Using both hands, Elizabeth pushed herself off and away from Darcy. As she rose up, he reached for the frog but missed, his hand grazing Elizabeth's bosom. They both blushed profusely as the frog, seizing the moment, jumped down Elizabeth's décolletage.

Grasping to restrain the cat, Darcy wedged his fingers under the animal's red and gold collar. With an unearthly yowl, the cat broke free from his grip; his yellow eyes now twice their size, the enlarged pupils focused on Elizabeth's bodice where the frog had sought refuge. The cat lunged for her chest.

Darcy grabbed the feline by the scruff of the neck, and although it fought viciously, he was able to deposit it into the garden. Clicking the door firmly behind him, he returned to Elizabeth while blotting the scratches on his hands.

Wishing to clear her good name, Elizabeth spoke first. "I was not snooping. I promise. The box was about to fall off the shelf. I had to save it! It fell into my hands!"

She felt the frog cuddle between her breasts. The feeling, though slimy, was not at all cold, but it was weird.

"May I have my frog?" Darcy extended his hand. A dimple tweaked, as he drew his firm masculine lips into a stern but appealing thin line.

Elizabeth sensed that his thoughts lingered on their most recent position on the floor. She blushed, turned away, and extracted the reluctant frog from her bosom, prying his frog-toes from the lace edge of the neckline of her chemise.

Holding the creature between her thumb and index finger, she returned the scamp to Darcy.

"Since you have gone to so much trouble to save my

frog, I shall tell you about him." Darcy attempted to look sincere, but Elizabeth sensed she was not about to hear the truth.

"This is my lucky frog, Georgie. He traveled with me from London. I must keep him hidden from Miss Bingley as she loathes all creatures, but most particularly frogs." He rubbed the frog's head and it purred. "I fear she would do him harm."

"Why did you put his box in such a precarious position on that high shelf?"

He looked sheepish. "It was not safe to leave Georgie in the desk, no matter that it was locked, as Miss Bingley might come prying before I returned. I dashed into the garden for what I thought would be a brief run for water and flies for Georgie's dinner. Unfortunately it is late in the season and flies are scarce. It took me longer than I thought."

"You should have known any self-respecting frog can move a box on a shelf! Next time try to be more careful."

"Thank you for saving him. Would you be so kind as to stay here with him while I return to the garden for more flies as the others have escaped?"

"And what of that nasty cat? Is that a Netherfield cat? He seems quite vicious."

"He stowed away in our carriage, most likely when

we left London. He would have eaten my frog, or at the least run off with him."

Darcy's gaze was such that it would have melted a lesser lady. "Please tell me if there is any way I can repay you for saving Georgie from a most inglorious end."

"I prefer you be beholding to me. Perhaps someday I shall call on your offer." She thought to ask about Fiona Feelgood, but she knew all there was to know. Darcy was to meet with the witch the morning after Bingley's ball.

CHAPTER SEVENTEEN
GEORGIE

"I must collect more flies before poor Georgie starves. I shall close the door tightly behind me. If that cat returns, do not be reluctant to throw a book at him."

Elizabeth could not put aside the thought that Darcy was not being completely honest with her. But why should he be, since he had already declared her not magical enough for him?

Once Darcy had stepped outside, Elizabeth opened the box, as she felt sorry for the poor frog. He blinked, adjusting his eyes to the candlelight. She extended her hand to pet him and he leaned forward pressing his frog lips to her hand. She found him to be a rather courtly amphibian.

Darcy returned with a small bowl of water and a second bottle of flies. Elizabeth dipped her fingers in the water and sprinkled it on Georgie's head. She gave him a gentle massage as he caught the dripping water with his elongated tongue.

Once Georgie had been watered down, Darcy let a fly loose near the frog's mouth. The insect vanished in a single slurp.

Elizabeth squinted her eyes questioningly as Darcy described a childhood spent catching frogs in the ponds on his Pemberley estate. She had the strange feeling he was trying to justify Georgie's presence as he painted a childhood layered with happy memories.

The frog rolled over and Elizabeth splashed his belly with water, smiling at the little fellow.

Darcy grew uncomfortable with the fondness Elizabeth exhibited toward the frog. "I believe that is enough, Georgie." He righted the frog and attempted to return him to his box. But the green imp would have none of it. He spread his long skinny legs, gripping the outside of the box and refusing to be contained. With some maneuvering, and unbending of his little frog toes, Darcy soon had him settled in and the box snapped shut.

Elizabeth laughed, amused at a grown man wrestling with a frog.

Darcy regarded her with pleasure, "Has anyone ever told you that you have fine eyes?" he said.

For an instant Elizabeth thought he was speaking to the frog as the compliment came so unexpectedly. An uneasy feeling seeped into her heart. Jane often cautioned her about finding the bad where none existed and yet she could not help but feel that Mr. Darcy meant trouble and a disruption of her quiet life in Longbourn. She vowed to step back from the web this charming man was weaving.

***

The following day, Elizabeth and Jane were once again in their shared bedroom at Longbourn. Fully recovered and happy to be at home, despite her longing for Mr. Bingley, Jane sat in the window seat, while her owl perched on the sill, nuzzling his head against her cheek.

Pyewacket snuggled in Elizabeth's lap snoozing. She stroked his fur finding it a calming distraction from the worry that built like a storm within her. "I must find Fiona Feelgood and caution her, for I fear Mr. Darcy and Mr. Bingley will trick her into telling all. She is easily duped," Elizabeth said. "This is what comes from helping a Limited Liability Witch."

"Fiona is a dear," Jane said. "Her love spells have an *almost* perfect record."

"I trust you did not employ her to enchant Mr. Bingley?" Elizabeth said.

"Of course not! I do not need a spell, as we are both truly and most sincerely in love."

We shall see, Elizabeth thought. She waited until after dinner, and then she set out to have a chat with Miss Fiona Feelgood. The ground had thoroughly dried and the air smelled of spring as she trudged to the northern border of the Longbourn estate.

She knocked on the door of Broom Cottage for exactly three minutes, but Miss Feelgood did not answer. Had she gone off with Mr. Darcy, not waiting until the day after the ball? Elizabeth stepped cautiously around the cottage and into the garden to see if Fiona was gardening.

Elizabeth shuddered as she saw her handy work still standing in the flowerbed. Swallowing back her guilt, she headed back to Longbourn.

CHAPTER EIGHTEEN
BINGLEY'S BALL

Elizabeth entered the drawing room at Netherfield, wearing a pale pink gown, her dark hair pinned in an upsweep and dotted with baby's breath. Jane was a vision in light blue, her long blonde hair held off her swan-like neck with a swirl of ribbon. The two youngest sisters followed, chattering in the manner of children with no thought for how frivolous they appeared.

A group of red-coated militia stood chatting and assessing the arriving ladies. Standing within the center of the group was a tall, rather handsome man with long dark hair, wisps of which rested on the black and gold collar of his red uniform.

Even at a distance, Elizabeth noted that his eyes glowed with a greenish-yellow aura. There was something vaguely familiar about him. He beamed in on Elizabeth with those extraordinary eyes and sauntered toward her with a swagger to his hips.

She had dressed with more than usual care, and prepared in the highest spirits for the conquest of all in attendance, but there was torment in Elizabeth's soul, for she was conflicted. Darcy had her interest as no man had before and yet, his peculiar behavior left her unsettled. His devotion to a frog—not that there was anything wrong with frogs—was curious. Not many men with his resources would choose an amphibian as a pet.

"I would, under normal circumstances, wait for a proper introduction, but since I must leave immediately, I shall be so bold as to make the acquaintance of the loveliest lady in the room," he said.

Elizabeth smiled. "I would be happy to present you to my sister Jane; but you and I have never been properly introduced. You remain a stranger to me," she spoke teasingly.

"I was referring to you. You are the loveliest lady here," he said taking her hand and kissing it lightly. "I feel as if I have known you all my life, and so forgive me, for you are correct. We have never been properly introduced. Had I the time, I would find a mutual acquaintance and plead an introduction from that person. But since I must leave momentarily, allow me the liberty of saying that I am George Wickham, formerly of Pemberley."

Pemberley? Darcy's estate? Was that why he looked familiar? "Are you related to Fitzwilliam Darcy?" she asked.

"I fear if the gentleman heard your question, he would choke with rage. And now, unfortunately, I must dash. Fitzwilliam Darcy will be descending the stairs at any moment."

Elizabeth looked to the staircase but no one was there. When she looked back, Mr. Wickham had vanished. Odd.

She was disappointed, as she wished a diversion from Mr. Darcy; a conversation with the handsome Mr. Wickham would have been an appropriate excuse. She could not remove the thought that Darcy was a witch hunter, perhaps testing her with the frog, as witches are partial to frogs. Had her comfort with the green hoppy creature revealed too much? Most ladies would have squealed in revulsion. A witch would not.

Elizabeth resolved against any meaningful dialogue with Darcy. She sensed that if she let her guard down he might win her heart, discover her secret, and betray her for the bounty on witches. And yet, was he not reputed to be one of the wealthiest men in England? Why would he require the small bounty attached to a simple country witch? Elizabeth was thoroughly confused. If she were not careful, both she and Jane would be doomed. The man might already have Miss Feelgood in his clutches.

As Darcy approached, she quickly accepted a dance with Colonel Forster. Elizabeth stepped onto the floor, knowing Darcy's eyes were upon her with a heat that bore through her, causing her great discomfort.

When the dance was over, the colonel escorted her to Jane's right side; Mr. Bingley clung to Jane's left side like moss on a shadowed tree. Elizabeth quickly engaged herself in animated conversation with her sister in the hopes Darcy would not interfere, but he did.

Mr. Darcy took her by surprise in his application for her hand and without knowing what she did, she accepted the next two dances from him. Turning abruptly, he walked away.

Elizabeth fretted over her own want of presence of mind. This was the first time in her life that she had regretted her legacy.

Mr. Bingley excused himself from Jane's side.

"Let us walk," Elizabeth said to her sister. "My lips are parched from smiling."

The sisters strolled to the refreshment table and Elizabeth accepted a glass of lemonade. "I cannot dance with that man!" she said, holding the drink to her mouth to conceal her frown.

Jane tried to console her. "I dare say you will find Mr. Darcy agreeable."

"That is what I am afraid of, for I am sure he is a witch hunter, both he and his friend, Mr. Bingley. They will collect a bounty for turning us in to the London Anti-Magic Tribunal."

"Mr. Bingley is too kind-hearted to be a hunter. Why, he can barely bring himself to kill a bug."

"I have always felt we were safe to practice our craft discreetly in the country, but perhaps London has become lean pickings for bounty hunters and they are now searching the shires," Elizabeth said.

"You worry much too much. You shall grow furrows between your brows," Jane teased a smile from her sister.

Glancing around to be sure no one might hear them, Elizabeth spoke. "We have not received a letter from Aunt Gardiner in a fortnight. I am truly worried. Living in Wapping puts Aunt and Uncle Gardiner at great risk. While our magic has grown stronger from our freedom and fresh air, they must endure constant scrutiny and soot. I hope their skills have not withered from lack of use."

"Darcy is staring at you," Jane whispered. "Please take the glass away from your mouth and smile. Dance with the man. I dare say you will find him very agreeable."

Elizabeth flushed recalling the *very* agreeable sensations of falling on top of Mr. Darcy. She had not shared her embarrassment with Jane. Proper manners dictated that she should have removed herself from Darcy promptly. Did he think her wanton for remaining in place for those long, lovely moments? Or did he understand that she was stunned and unable to move?

"That is what I fear, finding him agreeable! Do you not sense his true vocation to be that of a witch hunter?"

"Do not wish us such an evil," Jane said. She pinched her sister's arm. "Your judgment on occasion has been wrong. You guessed Mrs. Graham to be a witch hunter when she arrived in Meryton and you put that itching spell on her."

"Do not remind me for I still have nightmares of that poor lady scratching and scratching. I cannot bear to greet her in church for the guilt of my actions. To think, I put a spell on her merely because she was a stranger with a curious mind.

Elizabeth and Jane had inherited their magic skills from their maternal grandmother. And although Jane took the powers as a blessing, Elizabeth had mixed opinions. She remained ever cognizant of Grandma Pansy's warnings, and had a tendency to suspect witch hunters behind every new face.

CHAPTER NINETEEN
FUN WITH FEATHERS

Acceptance of witches had changed since Grandma Pansy Gardiner's day. The penalties were not as severe as they had been during the last century. Elizabeth often wondered if her grandmother had placed a spell upon her father—how else would he have been swept off his feet and enchanted enough to ask for her mother's hand? Fanny Bennet had been on the circuit long after her prime years and witchcraft must have been involved in their union.

Mrs. Bennet had not inherited her mother's abilities, and in obedience to their grandmother's wishes, Jane and Elizabeth told absolutely no one of the gifts, except for Miss Feelgood, and of course, their aunt and uncle. It had been difficult keeping the secret from their family, but a promise was a promise. Grandma Pansy had made them swear on their hearts they would not tell their mother, as she would coerce them into using their gifts for her own ends.

Miss Bingley approached the sisters in a cloud of orange silk. Her arrival shook Elizabeth from her thoughts. "It appears that Mr. Darcy has asked you for a dance, Miss Bennet. I would not get too close to the man, for his heart belongs to another. I would hate to see you disappointed."

"Really? Is the lady someone in London society?" Elizabeth asked, mildly relieved.

"Yes and no. I will tell you." She put her finger to her lips. "He is secretly in love with me." She winked.

"That *is* a well-kept secret, as I believe Mr. Darcy himself is not aware of his affections for you."

"He will be," she said, just as she felt a tickle below her lip.

"You have a feather on your chin," Elizabeth said.

Caroline Bingley's hand came up so quickly she smacked herself. "I must excuse myself!" And with her hand on her chin, she scurried away to pluck the feather in private.

"Well done!" Elizabeth said to Jane, once they were alone. Elizabeth's giggles had an unpredictable effect on her skills. As she continued to titter, the glass of lemonade slipped from her hand and floated in midair for an instant before she snatched it back and placed it on the table.

Having sworn off witchcraft after the debacle with the hermit, Elizabeth feared this little mistake might expose her, as she caught Darcy watching the lemonade glass with a most curious expression.

CHAPTER TWENTY
MR. COLLINS

Elizabeth listened with delight to the happy though modest hopes that Jane entertained for Mr. Bingley's regard. She encouraged her sister's beliefs in the gentleman's affections.

Mr. Bingley returned to Jane's side and his warmth of feelings for her lit the ballroom. Elizabeth excused herself to leave the couple to their privacy. She joined her best friend, Charlotte Lucas, who stood alone appearing forlorn. Elizabeth had only just begun to speak of the ball when her odious cousin, the rector Mr. Collins inserted his chubby body between the ladies.

"Miss Elizabeth, I must tell you my most exciting news!" All things were exciting to the rector, with the exception of his own tedious sermons, which were as stimulating as a funeral dirge. Elizabeth grit her teeth ready to endure his latest thrill, as this windbag was heir to the Bennet estate and would someday own her beloved Longbourn. Prudence dictated she give him a polite listen.

He began in a most animated manner, spittle flying from his lips, which reminded Elizabeth of two plump worms. "I have just made the most amazing discovery! There is now in this room a near relation of my patroness, Lady Catherine de Bourgh! Is that not serendipitous?"

Elizabeth bit her lip. Serendipitous was not the word she would have chosen, for Mr. Collins was the finest example of a sycophant that she could imagine. The man lived in a bubble of worship for his patroness, the dowager Lady Catherine, a most pompous and dictatorial person.

"Who would have thought of my meeting with Mr. Fitzwilliam Darcy, a nephew of Lady Catherine de Bourgh, in this ball! I am so glad I made this discovery, for I will pay my respects to him. Once I have impressed myself upon him, he will no doubt mention my earnest personality to his aunt."

Elizabeth gasped. "You are not going to introduce yourself to Mr. Darcy!"

Charlotte excused herself as she sensed an argument. Her friend was not known to refrain from correcting those she thought to be foolish.

As she stepped away, Jane joined Elizabeth, sensing the need for her lightness of mood.

Mr. Collins eyes grew large in surprise at Elizabeth's audacity in correcting him. "Of course I am going to introduce myself. And I will apologize for not having spoken to him earlier. I have no doubt he will be pleased to hear that, as of last week, Lady Catherine was in fine health."

What Mr. Collins intended to do was an impertinent liberty outside the scope of common etiquette. For a rector, her cousin was sorely ignorant of proper conduct. If either man spoke first it should be Mr. Darcy, the superior in consequence, to begin the acquaintance. It was very presumptuous of a man of lesser rank to be so forward.

Elizabeth tried to dissuade her cousin from his scheme. To his credit he listened to her, and when she had ceased speaking, he replied.

"My dear Miss Elizabeth, I have the highest opinion of your excellent judgment in all matters within the extent of your experience. But you must understand that there is a wide difference between established etiquette for the laity and those that govern the clergy. I am welcome where others may not approach."

The man was a fool but too full of himself to notice. Elizabeth exchanged a wink with Jane and a feather appeared on Mr. Collins' chin with a *poof*.

"I can assure you that I will maintain the proper amount of humility. But do know that I consider the clerical office as equal in dignity with the highest rank in the kingdom. So pardon me if I do not accept your advice in this matter." With a low bow and a feather on his chin, he left Elizabeth and Jane, and set out to attack Mr. Darcy.

Nudging Jane's elbow Elizabeth said, "Let us move closer for this should be amusing."

They were unable to stand close enough to hear, but they did watch their cousin as he executed a solemn bow and saw his lips motion the words, "apology," "Hunsford," and "Lady Catherine de Bourgh." It was an embarrassment to see the Bennet name upon those wormy lips.

"Still there!" Jane said, noting the feather on his chin. "I am getting rather good at chin feathers."

Mr. Darcy eyed the rector with puzzlement, and when at last Mr. Collins broke off his litany of compliments, Mr. Darcy spoke with civil disdain.

Mr. Collins began again, not the least bit discouraged by Mr. Darcy's obvious revulsion at his behavior. Elizabeth could see the tension forming in Mr. Darcy's face as his jaws clenched and his eyes focused above Mr. Collins' bobbing head, unable to bring himself to make eye contact with the little rodent.

The instant the clergyman paused, Mr. Darcy made a slight bow and moved away. Mr. Collins returned to Elizabeth and Jane, with the feather still poking from his chin.

"That went very well!" he said. "Mr. Darcy was most pleased with my attention. He even went so far as to compliment Lady Catherine's discernment in selecting me for Hunsford parish. Upon the whole, our conversation went as I told you it would. Clergymen do possess a certain unique status."

"I have learned something new this day. And I am sure Mr. Darcy will long remember your meeting." Elizabeth turned away as she spoke for fear of breaking into giggles as the feather had grown by an inch. She whispered to her sister, "Enough!"

She felt almost as happy as Jane watching Mr. Bingley beam when he drew near. Elizabeth imagined them happily married, living in Netherfield and raising a family of blue-eyed, blond-headed children. She wondered if Grandma Pansy's gift for magic would pass to Jane's children. Elizabeth could not bring herself to think of having children of her own, as she thought it impossible for her to ever love any man enough to forfeit her freedom.

Mrs. Bennet lounged on a loveseat holding court. She was bragging to Lady Lucas about Jane's marriage to the wealthy Mr. Bingley, notwithstanding that the gentleman had yet to ask for Jane's hand.

Elizabeth's stomach roiled at the sound of her mother's avaricious plans for the future. She felt it necessary to step away and breathe some fresh air. Mrs. Bennet's voice trailed after her as she loudly enumerated the advantages the Bennets would reap once Jane married Mr. Bingley. At that moment, Elizabeth wished to stuff her mother's mouth with feathers. But she would leave the feathers for Jane.

She did not know that at that very moment, Mr. Darcy fought an overwhelming urge to turn Mrs. Bennet into a goose for she possessed all the qualities of such a bird: she was plump, she honked, and she waddled.

CHAPTER TWENTY-ONE
DARCY'S FAVOR

When the dancing recommenced, Darcy approached to claim her hand. Jane whispered to Elizabeth, cautioning her not to be a simpleton, for she had no proof that he was a witch hunter.

Reluctantly, Elizabeth took her place in the dance, amazed at the gossip she incited by standing with Mr. Darcy as her partner. She read in her neighbors' looks, their amazement in beholding her dancing with Darcy, as he had made himself quite unpopular within the Meryton assemblage.

For some time Darcy and Elizabeth moved around the floor without speaking a word. She began to imagine that their silence would endure through the two dances, which suited her purpose, as he would not be able to trick her into a revealing conversation or placing her foot in her open mouth.

As they touched hands, she did not have to look up

to feel his admiring looks. She remembered his tenderness with the frog. Perhaps she had misjudged Mr. Darcy, for surely a man who treated his frog with such kindness could not be a witch hunter. She determined to engage him in polite banter as he was trying so hard to curry her favor. So she remarked on the dance.

Darcy replied, and was again silent. After a pause of some minutes, she addressed him a second time. "It is your turn to say something now, Mr. Darcy. I talked about the dance, and you ought to make some sort of remark on the size of the room, or the number of couples."

"My mind is occupied with concerns for Georgie," he said. "He is locked away, but I must keep Miss Bingley within my sights. Have you seen her recently?"

"I believe she is tending to her chin."

He appeared confused. "I beg your pardon?"

"I said she just walked in." Elizabeth nodded toward the alcove near the ladies parlor.

"Then I must go check on Georgie as soon as this dance is over."

"Very well. I understand. Have you secured your frog? Is he safe from that black cat? I imagine that the owner of such a fine animal, wearing such an expensive collar, must not now be frantic to find him."

"You think that mangy cat is a fine animal? Let us not speak of it now. But I will ask a favor of you later, when we are in a more private setting," Darcy said, his face took on a serious look.

And still she could think of nothing else but that he wanted to get her alone to discern if she was in fact a witch. And so she set about to discipline herself to believe that she did not possess magic. She remained silent as they stepped through the final movements of the dance.

"Have you changed your mind and decided not to talk while you are dancing?" Darcy said, concerned that he had offended her. "For I can understand that anyone could overhear our conversation and there are some things that must be private."

"One must speak a little, you know," she said. "It would look odd to be entirely silent for half an hour together. A little conversation goes a long way." And with that she tripped over the hem of her dress, miss stepping as she spoke.

"I can see why you do not wish to dance and talk at the same time. It is rather a risky procedure for you, is it not?" he said with a delighted smirk.

"It must be wonderful to be so perfect," Elizabeth said. "I see a great similarity in the turn of our minds. We are each of an unsocial, taciturn disposition, unwilling to speak unless we expect to say something that will amaze the whole room and be handed down to posterity."

"I am not sure we are so similar, for you think you must prove yourself in all interactions, whereas I do not require validation from strangers," he said, a bit too snippy.

Elizabeth took his arm in step with the other couples, "I believe you have just insulted me, sir."

"It was not intentional, but rather a response to your directness. You are quick to analyze the actions of others but you do not accept a critique of your own behavior."

Elizabeth sighed. "Let us just dance, for we have tried two or three subjects already without success, and what we are to talk of next I cannot imagine."

"What think you of books?" said he, smiling. "Do you find them a way of avoiding conversation?"

She thought of the dueling book. Was he again teasing her? "I am sure we never read the same book, or not with the same feelings."

"I am sorry you think so; but if that be the case, there can at least be no want of subject. We may compare our different opinions and argue our points."

"No, I cannot talk of books in a ballroom; my head is always full of the dancing."

"Are you counting the steps?" he asked, playfully, for he was beginning to understand her teasing and found it refreshing.

"Yes, always," she replied, without knowing what she said, for her thoughts had wandered to Mr. Wickham and his hasty exit. What was the hostility between the two men? Wickham claimed to have spent his childhood at Pemberley. Could that be true?

"I recall hearing you once say, Mr. Darcy, that you hardly ever forgave, that your resentment, once created, was unappeasable. I had the pleasure of a very brief chat with Mr. Wickham before you arrived. When he sensed your coming, he ran off with his tail between his legs.

Darcy turned pale, and his eyes grew hooded. "That would be a perfect description of George Wickham— a man with his tail permanently between his legs."

"You are very cautious, I suppose, as to those you take on in friendship?"

"I am," said he, quite firmly.

"And you never allow yourself to be blinded by prejudice?"

"I hope not," he said.

"It is particularly incumbent on those who never change their opinion, to be secure of judging properly at first," Elizabeth said.

"May I ask where you are going with these questions?"

"I am trying to understand why Mr. Wickham ran off at the mere thought of your approach."

"Of what concern is that to you?" he asked.

She shook her head. "I do not understand. I hear such different accounts of you that puzzle me exceedingly."

"I can readily believe," he answered gravely, "that reports may vary greatly with respect to me, and I could wish, Miss Bennet, that you would not sketch my character at the present moment, as there is reason to fear that the performance would reflect no credit on either of us. You do not know me well enough."

"But I may never have another opportunity, for you and Mr. Bingley may leave Netherfield as quickly as you arrived."

"Why would we leave when we have only just arrived?" he asked.

"Call it a precognition, if you will. I have a sense of the future and I feel you will be leaving us shortly."

"That sounds like a threat." Once again he smirked. "When this dance is over, let us step outside. I would ask a favor of you, before I disappear."

"What of your frog?" she asked.

"He will not be joining us."

Elizabeth could not help but laugh. "That is not what I meant. I thought you wished to keep Georgie from Caroline Bingley? Can we not adjourn to the library to check on your frog?"

CHAPTER TWENTY-TWO
BEWARE OF WICKHAM

But even as she suggested that they be alone, she realized the error of her thought. To be unaccompanied with Darcy was to court danger in more ways than she cared to count.

"Should we dare leave the party and step into a room, closing the door behind us, your reputation would be instantly worthless. I will not allow anyone to say an unkind word about you," he said.

Darcy knew he was developing a powerful feeling for this Hertfordshire lass. But his caring could go no further, for they were of different worlds, and with his mother's legacy to honor, he could take no wife...even one who could make a glass of lemonade float.

The dance ended, and they had not long separated when Miss Bingley came toward Elizabeth, and with an expression of civil disdain, accosted her. "I see you have danced *two* dances in my absence. Do not think

I am ignorant of your plans, but Fitzwilliam Darcy is beyond your reach."

Thinking to make Miss Bingley hush, Elizabeth rubbed her finger under her own chin as one would to signal a friend who was unaware of a spot of sauce on her face.

Turning crimson, the woman cupped her chin and scurried back to the ladies parlor to check her face for feathers.

Jane slipped to her sister's side. "I asked Mr. Bingley about Mr. Wickham and Mr. Darcy. But I have nothing satisfactory to tell you. He does not know the man's entire history or why Mr. Darcy hates him so. But as much as I dislike using that word, there is hate between them. Mr. Bingley does vouch for Mr. Darcy most highly and respects his wisdom in all matters, save one. And of that one matter, he would say nothing more than that we are all entitled to make a mistake."

"So that is all he would say?"

"Mr. Bingley's thoughts on Mr. Wickham can be summed up thus: he thinks

Mr. Wickham is not a respectable young man."

"I have not a doubt of Mr. Bingley's sincerity," said Elizabeth warmly; "but you must excuse my not being convinced by his assurances only. Mr. Bingley's defense of his friend was a very able one, I dare say, but since he is his loyal friend, I shall venture to still think of Mr. Wickham and Mr. Darcy as I did before."

Darcy returned to Elizabeth's side. "Miss Bennet, would you join me in partaking of some fresh air?" He bowed toward the veranda and she took his arm.

They crossed the room, stepping carefully around the dancers. He held the door and Elizabeth stepped out onto the balcony. The full moon smiled down on them with a mischievous face. Why *was* Mr. Darcy so eager to get her alone? He was blocking her ability to sense the future. She wasn't always accurate, but she could tell that this man was deliberately keeping her out of his thoughts and his future.

"I have a favor to ask," he said. "On the morrow, I must attend an important meeting. I do not wish to expose Georgie to the elements, as he is of a somewhat fragile nature. Bingley will be joining me and there is no one else I trust with my frog. Will you frog-sit for me?"

Elizabeth knew Mr. Darcy was meeting with Fiona Feelgood since she had eavesdropped on their plans while at Netherfield. But the love witch could not possibly introduce Herman the Hermit to Mr. Darcy; only the second eldest witch of Longbourn could do that. Elizabeth was not about to confess her skills to Mr. Darcy, a possible witch hunter. For all she knew his frog might be a decoy and the search for the hermit a mere ploy.

When she did not respond to his request, Mr. Darcy grew tense. "I do not wish to leave him anywhere in Netherfield as Miss Bingley is forever meddling, and that black cat continues to lurk. The loss of Georgie would pain me greatly," he said, his dark eyes twin pools inviting Elizabeth to dive in. Unable to refuse him, she nodded in agreement.

"Wonderful! I will bring him to you in the morning. He will have been watered and fed. Thank you!"

There was such sincerity in his request that she could not deny him. And so the time was appointed for the clandestine passing of the frog.

Elizabeth secretly resolved that Darcy would not meet with Fiona Feelgood without her observing them since she had to protect herself. And so despite her promise to keep Georgie in her bedroom, that night she prepared a basket to carry the frog to Broom Cottage on the morrow.

CHAPTER TWENTY-THREE
BROOM COTTAGE

The morning sun broke through the clouds just as Darcy and Bingley arrived at Longbourn. Elizabeth had been sitting in the window seat from before dawn, watching for their arrival.

She slipped from the window and tiptoed down the stairs barely making a sound. Inching out the front door, Elizabeth dashed down the steps and ran to where the men remained on their horses in the shadow of the trees, unseen by any early risers.

Darcy leaned down from his huge black stallion and carefully handed the green enamel box to Elizabeth. She tucked it under her shawl, wished them safe journey, and returned to her room.

Jane slept on, a pleased smile on her face. Perhaps she was dreaming of Mr. Bingley? Making sure the windows were securely closed, Elizabeth sat in the window seat and allowed Georgie to come out of his confinement. Staring deeply into his eyes, she said. "I see you as something more than a frog—not that there is anything wrong with being a frog. But exactly who are you?"

Georgie rubbed his cold snout against her hand, and lifted his little frog-toes to grasp her finger. "You are someone special. I understand it is of great importance to remove the spell, but only a hermit can undo the spell of a witch. I can un-spell my own magic, but not that of another witch." She stroked his little head. "You poor dear. Who did this to you? And why?"

Lifting the frog and placing him in a small straw picnic basket with lots of good ventilation, she said. "No matter, for I shall have you right as rain before the sun sets."

At that moment, her familiar, Pyewacket, strutted into the room. He placed his paws on Elizabeth's lap and looked with great curiosity at the basket. Unable to contain his feline inquisitiveness, he let out a Siamese cry that sounded much like a baby calling for his mother, and then he jumped up on the window seat.

Pyewacket prodded the basket with his nose, and moved the lid with his paws. All cats have an extraordinary sense of smell, but familiars possess skills far greater than the average feline. When he had satisfied his curiosity, he studied Elizabeth for an explanation.

"Yes, that is a frog you smell in the basket," she said, lowering her voice. "We must protect this little fellow. I trust you to help me guard Georgie for there is a black cat stalking him and it means to do him harm. The cat may be magical, so be prepared to defend."

Pyewacket blinked twice, as was his way as her familiar. She could trust him to carry out his guard duties. Elizabeth glanced over at the bed. Jane slept on. Taking a pen and paper, she left her sister an innocuous note, that said nothing except that she had gone for a stroll, which in fact, was the truth.

She adjusted the button fastener on the basket. "We must monitor Mr. Darcy's scheme to meet with Miss Feelgood," she whispered to the Pyewacket.

Grabbing her shawl, Elizabeth put the basket on her arm and eased out the door in clear defiance of her promise to Mr. Darcy. She knew of a shortcut and should arrive minutes before the men on horseback.

With the handle of the basket containing the frog draped comfortably over her arm, Elizabeth hid in the shrubbery near the door of Broom Cottage, and watched Mr. Darcy and Mr. Bingley mount the three steps to the porch. Before Darcy could raise the brass knocker, the door flew open.

Miss Fiona Feelgood stood in the doorway, dressed in full storybook witch's attire. If she was trying to justify her reward by looking the part of a witch, she was playing a dangerous hand. Mr. Darcy and Mr. Bingley could easily lift her up and carry her away as the sign upon her door was sufficient to have her charged with witchcraft. It was rather risky for her to declare herself in business as *Love Witch, Ltd.* when bounty hunters were roaming the shires.

"Duck!" she yelped. "I just cast a spell and it's gotten away from me. The silly thing is springing about and—*slam!* The door closed in their faces. "One moment!" she trilled from behind the door. "I almost have it contained."

After a few thumps and some bumps the door re-opened. Miss Feelgood stood there sticking her hair under her witch's cap. "That's better, now where were we? Oh yes, I am prepared to tell you where the hermit is. I cannot vouch for his condition and he may not be able to offer you any assistance. Sad case that he is."

She addressed Darcy. "As to my reward. Within the pages of your mother's book of spells is a rose pressed flat from many years of hiding. I wish that dried rose as my reward."

Darcy stepped back, stunned. "How do you come to know of my mother's book?"

Fiona Feelgood tittered. "Everyone knows of Lady Anne Darcy, the most powerful but kindest witch that ever graced the shires. Her book is legend, as is the crushed rose said to protect a witch from her own spells. As you can see, I dearly need it."

"But why should I give it to you?" Darcy asked. "Perhaps I shall have use of it in the future."

The little witch cackled. "After this adventure, I doubt you will be bold enough to cast any more spells. Whereas I have a growing problem with mine, they keep bouncing back on me."

"You must tell me more of this hermit before I consider giving you my mother's rose. Mother must have had a good reason to keep the token."

"It was not always your mother's token. She confiscated it from a bad witch." She grinned a taunting grin. "You know the man—he was a child then—George Wickham."

"That blackguard is a witch?" Darcy said, staggering from this news since he and Wickham had grown up under the same roof and played together as boys. His enemy gave no sign of being a witch.

"How do you think Wickham came to be in your world at Pemberley? Do you not know of the cuckoo bird? He enters a friend's home, subverts his friend's parents to his own greedy end, making them believe he is needy, and in doing so the parents neglect their own biological offspring. Does this not sound familiar?"

"Bloody hell! Wickham is a cuckoo!"

"He carried a red rose to protect himself from his own spells. When your mother discovered the rose, she took it and placed it in her book of spells to discourage him from casting incantations. The legend says that no one but Lady Anne's heir can open the book and retrieve the rose," Miss Feelgood said. "And only the rose can unlock self-inflicted spells."

"Under my current circumstances I can promise to give you the rose. Now tell us where to find the hermit."

"Follow me," she said, stepping onto the path and heading to her garden.

Elizabeth knew at that moment that explanations would be forthcoming and that the secret she and Jane kept for twenty plus years would soon be exposed.

"Halt!" the high-pitched voice of Mr. Collins cut through the air. He quickly waddled to the threesome, elbowing his way between Mr. Darcy and Mr. Bingley; he grabbed Miss Feelgood by the arm.

"I am arresting you in the name of the London Anti-Magic Tribunal. Now come along quietly and it will go easy on you, Miss Feelgood," he said in a rather excited blather.

126

Fiona Feelgood struggled to pull away from his grasp. "You have no proof of my being a witch!" she said.

"You have a sign on your front door offering your services as a love witch!" he snapped, frustrated that she would argue the point.

"Poo! I am a love counselor; the term 'witch' is merely a way to attract business, for who does not wish to meet a witch? There is a renewed interest in magic you know," she said, wrinkling her nose as if to conjure a spell.

Elizabeth could not let the little witch be taken, or for that matter let one of her spells bounce back at her. Impulsively she stepped out from hiding. "Unhand that lady, you toad!"

Seeing Elizabeth now joining ranks against him, Mr. Collins realized he was outnumbered. Mr. Darcy, Mr. Bingley and his cousin, Miss Bennet could prevent him from carrying off the little witch. "I am here on the authority of the crown," he said, his voice quavering.

Mr. Collins looked from one to the other beseechingly. "It is not the money, not the bounty, you understand. It is the principle of the thing."

"I think not," Darcy snarled. "You will leave Miss Feelgood's property immediately."

Even if Mr. Collins left Miss Feelgood this day, he might come back on another afternoon bringing reinforcements. Elizabeth knew there was only one way to protect Fiona. She pointed her finger at the rector and chanted "Sotted, spotted, potted plant!"

Mr. Collins shuddered twice, shimmied once, and turned into a rather unattractive potted plant.

Darcy stared at Elizabeth with a look of both esteem and confusion. "A potted plant?" he said. "Is that the best you can do?"

"I am not good under pressure. Now quickly, let us get on with it." She looked at Darcy's bemused expression. "Yes, I am a witch, but I intend to cut back. And if you are a witch hunter, you shall not take me to London without a fight."

Fiona Feelgood studied their faces, thinking she saw a twinkle in Darcy's eyes. Could it be because he had not ducked when her latest love spell ran amuck? She gathered herself together and continued, "As I was saying, come with me."

Elizabeth adjusted the basket on her arm and stepped behind the little witch. The men followed the women into the garden. Darcy's mind tossed like a ship at sea. He suspected that Elizabeth was a witch and now it was confirmed. But all the witches he had met in his worldly travels had a way about them—a hunger, a blood-thirst. Miss Elizabeth Bennet exhibited none of these things. She was a piece of delightful magic, in an irritating way. He drove the romantic thoughts from his mind, for he had a kingdom to save.

CHAPTER TWENTY-FOUR
THE SPELL

Miss Feelgood trotted through the flowerbeds, and stopped in front of a garden gnome made of stone. "Meet Herman the Hermit."

Mr. Bingley was rendered speechless. Mr. Darcy sputtered angrily, "This is a trick! If this is the hermit he is of no use to me in this condition." He smacked the top of the stone gnome's head.

"Ouch!" the gnome yelped. For at that very instant Elizabeth wiggled her finger and released the hermit from her stoned gnome spell.

All but Elizabeth jumped at the cry coming from the former stone figure, now a live hermit.

"This is your handiwork?" Darcy asked Elizabeth. "I have known of accomplished ladies who can speak three languages while doing needlepoint, but this...this is a bit much!"

A mix of pride in her skills and prejudice against

Darcy' underestimation of a woman's skills caused Elizabeth to snap. "I have the ability to transform people into objects while simultaneously doing fine needlepoint and speaking in a rare Romanian dialect. In this case my spell was most necessary to stop Herman from—"

Miss Feelgood interrupted Elizabeth. "Herman came to me for a love spell, one which would make a certain lady fall in love with him," she said prying the hermit's arms from around her waist and mashing her foot onto his curly booted foot. He backed away, but not far.

"The spell I conjured for him bounced back on me, unfortunately. Herman is now besotted with me, but that was not his intention, nor mine. He had another lady in mind and wished to have *her* fall in love with *him*, not to be smitten himself, and certainly not with me! But now we are stuck with one another. Help us, please?"

With a consoling smile, Elizabeth continued. "When Miss Feelgood sent for my help in order to escape Herman's amorous advances, I performed the first thing that came to my mind when I could not undo her love spell. I turned the hermit into a garden gnome." She looked at the little man. "Sorry Herman."

The hermit rubbed his back. "You have no idea

how my back aches. Try standing in the rain for days on end."

"That is why I require your mother's rose," Miss Feelgood said to Darcy. "I have had too many spells bounce back on me lately. I am losing my touch. Despite my limited liability, I am not protected from my own magic. I fear I must close my business if this continues."

Darcy screwed his face in deep thought. "So my mother's rose undoes spells?"

Herman and Fiona shook their heads, "Only spells that bounce back on the witch. Self-inflicted spells."

Darcy sighed. "Then, you shall have the rose as promised, but only when I return to Netherfield."

Exhausted from the stress, Darcy wished for a more peaceful time. He found himself unable to take his eyes from Elizabeth. Her status as both the daughter of a gentleman and a witch were much below his and yet he wanted her as he had never wanted anything or anyone in his life. He felt a forever bond with Elizabeth. But would she have him with his pedigree? And would he be able to accept her family? His mind spun like a runaway wagon wheel.

Darcy addressed Herman. "It is my understanding that you can undo the spells of others. I tied a knot of a spell and require help to untangle it." His next word sent a chill through Elizabeth. "The fate of England is at stake."

Miss Feelgood held her arm up forcing Herman to keep his distance. The love in his watery blue eyes was too icky for her to tolerate and she looked away.

"For a hermit to undo a spell, he must know all the details of who, where, when, and most importantly why," Herman said. "The reason for undoing a spell must be purer than the reason for which it was first cast."

Elizabeth took a seat on a tiny stool, placing the basket next to her. She lifted the lid, and found Georgie looking up at her with huge worried eyes. Leaning into the basket, she whispered, "Please do not worry. I am protecting you. Let me hear Mr. Darcy's story."

"I shall begin at the beginning," Darcy began, "which commences in the Queen's House two weeks ago. The Prince Regent had invited me for dinner and advice. He had just begun to act in his father's stead as George III is now confined for his own safety. I am not breaking any confidences in sharing that the king was deemed insane. He was dicked in the nob and locked in the Tower."

Elizabeth was impressed with Mr. Darcy connections and understood that not only had he created some sort of royal mess, but that his social rank was so far above hers as to make an future for them an impossibility. He was close to royalty and she was not.

"The Prince Regent knew of my mother's skills in white magic and wished to have his reign begin with blessings from the church and the witches. He requested I perform a spell that would ensure he become a fair king. You must remember I had never performed a spell before."

Elizabeth opened the basket and looked down at the shinny green frog assuming where Darcy's tale was going. "So that is who you are! I am honored to have sprinkled your belly, your highness."

Darcy continued to share the truth of his blunder with the hermit. "Although I treasured my mother's book of spells, I had not attempted to use them. But when His Royal Highness asked for my assistance on behalf of king and country, I could not deny him the incantation. He wished to be a fair king, which seemed a decent request. And so I conjured, from my mother's book, what I thought would be the proper spell. Unfortunately, what I intended—a fair king—came out to be a frog king."

The hermit began to chuckle, finally tumbling over in a fit of laughter. Elizabeth and Fiona shared a look and then burst into snickers. Elizabeth's giggles levitated the basket from the stool, and it floated in the air with the lid popping open. Georgie jumped out and into Elizabeth's lap.

"I felt the request compromised my ethics and yet this was for king and country," Darcy said. "The Prince Regent convinced me that my mother would have wanted me to make him a fair king. But once I had turned him into a frog, I could not undo the spell. I panicked."

"How did you know to seek out a hermit?" Elizabeth asked.

"There was a footnote in my mother's book stating that when all else fails, see a hermit, preferably Herman in Hertfordshire."

"Pardon me, but this undoing is far too complicated!" Herman said. "Considering the parties involved and the risk, I must ask for something in payment."

Darcy looked at Elizabeth with a frown of frustration and then he returned his gaze to Herman. "What do you wish? A hyacinth that grants ever lasting life or a daisy that won't tell?" His words were sarcastic as he was not accustomed to dealing with magic and hermits and witches, oh my.

Stroking Georgie's head, Elizabeth wondered how she could help, for it was clear that Darcy, though gifted with a fine heritage in witchcraft, was unschooled and floundering.

CHAPTER TWENTY-FIVE
A RIDDLE

Herman straightened himself to his full four-and-twenty inches, cleared his stony throat and spoke. "I know! You must answer a riddle, for we hermits love riddles. It is our favorite thing besides falling in love. You will have three guesses and no more. Should you fail to answer correctly, you must take the frog back to London and place him in the throne. Then you must confess your sin. I am sure they will find a comfortable cell for you in the Black Tower."

The hermit cut his gaze from Darcy to the frog in Elizabeth's lap. "But if you answer correctly I will restore the Prince Regent to his human condition and long may he rule." He smiled, a piece of gravel falling from the corner of his mouth.

Bingley had taken to sitting on a rustic bench amid the petunias. Afflicted with a throbbing headache, he wanted no part of Darcy's stew and wished himself back in Jane's company. A riddle no less! He felt he had been a good friend, but this was more than he had bargained for and he refused to take part in the game.

"Go on," Darcy said to the hermit, oblivious to Bingley's attitude.

Clearing his throat, Herman recited his riddle. "What has no shape but takes many forms?"

Darcy stared at him. "That's the riddle? That simple ditty will restore the monarch to the throne?"

"Jolly right!" said the hermit. "And you have only three guesses which you must use *now*, or the Prince Regent will remain a frog. A toad on the throne would cause a bit of tizzy for England."

"He is not a toad, he's a frog," Elizabeth said.

Running his hand through his dark hair, Mr. Darcy spoke in frustration. "Let us save time. I would happily pay you any amount for your services."

The hermit took on the air of one who had been insulted. "I am a hermit. We don't deal in money or jewels; we deal in conundrums. Riddles and puzzles please us. We have no use for coin of the realm."

Elizabeth grasped Georgie in her hand as Darcy came to her side. "Do you know the answer?" he asked, his eyeballs spinning. He suddenly realized she held the soon-to-be king of England in her hand and he snapped. "What did you not understand about your promise to keep Georgie safe in Longbourn?" he barked.

Immediately defensive and with a tear forming in her eye, Elizabeth retorted. "He is safe with me! Aren't you, Georgie? Mr. Darcy, you clearly need me here. I shall do you no good huddling in my bedchamber."

The frog licked her hand in response.

If it were possible to be jealous of an amphibian, Darcy was, at that moment. Did the frog have designs upon the woman Darcy was now sure he must wed if he were ever to be happy? The fates were having their jollies with him.

"Think!" Elizabeth said. "What has no shape but takes many forms?"

Darcy stared at her with a blank expression, why did he have such trouble concentrating around this woman? Was it merely her fine eyes, or her petite figure or more? He forced his mind to focus on the riddle. "Fire?"

"Yes, that makes sense. Try fire, for surely it has many forms!" She shared a confident smile with Darcy.

Returning to the hermit, who was still being held at bay by Miss Feelgood, Darcy said, "Fire!"

The hermit rubbed his bearded chin. "That might be a good answer for some, but it is the wrong answer for me. It is not fire." He appeared quite pleased to be rejecting the response.

A wad of tension wedged in Darcy's throat. He could barely swallow as he returned to Elizabeth. "We must do better. Let us try for a second time."

The couple paced the garden with all romantic thoughts put aside as they sought an answer to the riddle. Poor Georgie grew dry and leathery in Elizabeth's hand. She placed the frog in the birdbath, but he merely sat there looking ill. His color had changed to a pale green.

"There is something wrong with Georgie! What kind of spell did you cast? For all spells have a downside. I pray he is not dying."

"I am unsure of the complications of the spell. I looked under conjures for kings, and cast what I thought was appropriate. This is my first, and last, spell. I would not have performed it if Georgie had not pressed me with questions of my patriotism and forced me to use my mother's magic."

"That is the answer to the riddle!" Elizabeth grabbed Darcy's arm. "Magic has no shape but takes many forms!"

"You are right!" Darcy exclaimed, planting a kiss on Elizabeth's lips. She was shocked by the kiss, but no more than he. It was an impetuous, scandalous, but delicious brush of lips. Since she did not seem to object, Darcy determined to return for more—later.

He approached the hermit who was still pressing his struggle to embrace Miss Feelgood.

"We have your answer!" Darcy said. "Now, you definitely promise you will change the Prince Regent back into his human form?"

"You have the promise of a hermit and that is as good as a leprechaun's gold," Herman responded momentarily ceasing his pursuit of Miss Feelgood.

Darcy straightened himself to his full height and looking down at the hermit, he announced, "What has no shape but takes many forms? Magic!"

Herman looked at Mr. Darcy with great disappointment. "You may be a very handsome young man, but you are not the most intelligent. You have one more chance." As he spoke, he grabbed the love witch in a most inappropriate way.

Miss Fiona Feelgood squealed at this touch. "Hurry! I cannot keep this fool off me for much longer!" She pushed Herman's amorous advances away.

Darcy had all he could do to control himself. He was overcome with the desire to pummel the little man. He walked back to Elizabeth shaking his head. "The answer is right before us, I just cannot see it."

Elizabeth had settled back on the stool with Georgie perched next to her. He looked more withered and less green as the minutes passed.

"England will be lost because of the slip of my tongue. Napoleon will mount a campaign against us the moment he hears our king is a frog."

A wave of pity washed over Elizabeth, for Darcy would surely be destroyed and his family driven into disgrace.

"I fear my feelings for you are clouding my reasoning," Darcy said. "I have come to care so much for you, I cannot think clearly." He wrung his face with his hands. "We have one more guess, love."

Elizabeth jumped from the stool, startling the frog. "That's it! The answer is love!"

His face lit up. "You are brilliant!"

Dashing back to the hermit, Darcy pronounced the third and final answer to the riddle. "What has no shape but takes many forms? The answer is love!"

Herman the Hermit grinned. "Bring me that frog and you shall have your prince, for that is the correct answer. Love has no shape but takes many forms."

Elizabeth cheered and reached down to grab Georgie, but before her fingers could touch his shriveled body, he was caught and carried off in the jaws of a black cat. The feline moved so quickly he was barely visible except for the glint of gold and red on his collar.

Elizabeth covered her mouth with both hands to muffle her scream.

CHAPTER TWENTY-SIX
A BLACK CAT

Darcy ran after the cat but it disappeared under a hedge before he could get close. "Oh my!" Elizabeth cried, "I believe that is that same black cat we encountered in Netherfield."

"That is no cat—that is George Wickham!" said Herman.

Elizabeth stared at the hermit as if he had lost his mind.

"Lady Anne Darcy cast a spell on him to rid the shires of his presence but he found a way to return using the phases of the moon as his portal. Every full moon he turns into a cat."

Elizabeth clutched her hands, and biting hard on her knuckles. "We must save Georgie from that fiend."

"Until Wickham returns to his mortal form, he will need a human to assist him. I doubt he will attempt to eat a frog that is under a spell," Herman said.

"Come with us, Herman," Darcy said. "If we catch Wickham you can untangle Darcy's spell and return the Prince Regent to human form."

Elizabeth touched Darcy's arm and a spark passed between them. "I am so sorry for bringing Georgie here. I followed to defend myself, for I did not wish you to think less of me when Fiona spilled the beans. I am innocent of most wrong doings."

"Are you trying to say you are *not* enjoying being a witch?" Mr. Darcy said.

Elizabeth placed her hands on her hips and looked up at him. "I *am* a witch, descended from a long line of Longbourn witches and proud of it!"

Nodding, Mr. Darcy accepted her answer. "Not to worry. We will find the Prince and Wickham."

He turned to Miss Feelgood. "I will give you the rose from my mother's book, when next we meet."

"You are not going without me," she said, applying a two-handed shove to the hermit that sent him stumbling along the path. "I would not miss this adventure for all the world."

Taking charge of the rescuers, Elizabeth instructed Darcy, "Fiona and I will go to Longbourn on the chance that Wickham has sought hiding in my home."

The thought occurred to Elizabeth that Lydia had been quite smitten with Wickham at the ball. If he remained in a cat-like state, then he would need a human assistant. Lydia would make the perfect tool, for she had the brain of a slug when it came to men.

Darcy mounted Parsifal, seating the hermit in front of him. Bingley followed and they galloped off for Netherfield.

Elizabeth felt sure that Wickham had run off to Longbourn, for her sisters and mother would be less inclined to suspect him of foul play. Soldiers were always welcomed at Longbourn, much to her father's consternation.

Wickham would avoid Netherfield as Miss Caroline Bingley had made her witch hunting passion clear to all. Elizabeth was sure the villain, with the frog in his mouth, was on his way to her home and would make use of her birdbrained sisters to destroy the monarchy and the Darcy name. The only Bennet she could count on was Jane—and Pyewacket.

Longbourn was quiet when Elizabeth and Fiona arrived. Everyone must be in Meryton. Elizabeth slipped in the front door and inched up the staircase with the love witch at her heels. She snuck into the bedroom she shared with Jane.

Deeply engrossed in a book, Jane jumped from her seat when Fiona said, "Hi Jane!"

"What are *you* doing here?" Not that you are not

welcome. For love witches are always cheered. But I am just surprised you made it to my bedchamber without my knowing."

Elizabeth had remained in the hallway calling for Pyewacket. When he did not appear, she came into the room. "Have you seen a black cat? Preferably one with a frog in his mouth?" Elizabeth said.

Jane squinted her eyes, sorting her sister's question. "No black cats. No frogs."

At that moment, Pyewacket sauntered into the room. He made one large circle, beginning and ending at Elizabeth feet. It was his signal that all was not well.

"Pyewacket wishes us to follow," Elizabeth said. And the three women walked in back of the cat as he slinked out the door. He worked his way to Lydia and Kitty's room, placing his paw on the closed door. Without knocking, Elizabeth entered the room.

Lydia sat in a heap on the floor at the foot of her bed. She was wrapped in a coverlet and near tears. She held the frog wrapped in a piece of muslin, her face wrinkled in distaste. "This is an awful present!" she whined.

Elizabeth extended her hands and gently took the frog from her. "How did this poor thing come to be here?"

"Lieutenant Wickham appeared in my room. I

thought I was dreaming. He stood over my bed while I was napping. He looked handsome in his red and black uniform, with all the lovely gold braid. You can see how I thought I might be dreaming."

She only then noticed Fiona standing behind Elizabeth and Jane. "Who is she?" Lydia asked.

"An old friend," Elizabeth said tersely. "Which way did Mr. Wickham go?"

"That is just the thing. One moment he was here and the next he vanished. That was why I was sure I had dreamed his presence, but then I looked down and I had a frog in my arms. What a nasty wedding gift. Did I mention he asked me to marry him?"

Fiona tugged on Elizabeth. "She is not safe here, she must come downstairs with us and wait for Herman."

"Ooo! Who is Herman?" Lydia asked.

"He is a bit old for you," Elizabeth said.

"Does he wear a uniform?" Lydia asked.

Thinking a spell was a better idea, Elizabeth blinked twice at her youngest sister. Lydia curled up in a ball and fell fast asleep. They would be sure to inform her that she dreamed the entire thing.

Fiona, Jane, and Elizabeth settled into the parlor to await the arrival of the men. Elizabeth provided a bowl of water for Georgie while she told Jane of all that she missed. Her sister was happy to learn that Mr. Bingley would be joining them shortly.

Georgie managed to recover some of his coloring, and was now a pleasant shade of leaf green.

Unable to find Wickham at Netherfield, the men were now just arriving at Longbourn. Elizabeth held her breath, silently praying her Mr. and Mrs. Bennet would not return before they had sorted out the Prince Regent.

CHAPTER TWENTY-SEVEN
TA DA!

The men adjourned, taking the frog into Mr. Bennet's library to allow for privacy. After a bit of yowling and some unintelligible words, Herman emerged from the room, wiping the sweat from his brow. "These royal spells are the hardest to remove," he said.

Darcy stepped into the parlor. "We will need some clothing for the Prince," he said.

"I shall see what I can appropriate from our father's wardrobe," Jane said. She dashed up the stairs with Bingley close behind.

"Thank you for your help," Darcy said to Herman. "If you will wait a bit, I will take you home."

"I have seen too many people today. I am a hermit and prefer my own company. No offense but I shall be off." He faded into a mist before he reached the front door.

Try as they might, Elizabeth and Jane caught only

a passing glimpse of the Prince Regent as he rushed to the door dressed in Mr. Bennet's finest. At the threshold, he paused and turned as if to speak to them. The Prince locked eyes with Elizabeth for an instant and gave her a weak smile of thanks. His days under Darcy's spell had been most tiring, and he was needed in London. He must return to the palace by morning as England was in turmoil over his disappearance.

Bingley excused himself rather hurriedly, and Fiona disappeared in a poof. That left Jane and Elizabeth to explain to their father how the soon-to-be King of England had absconded with his Sunday best suit.

CHAPTER TWENTY-EIGHT
THE PROPOSAL

Shortly thereafter, Bingley, along with Miss Bingley and Mr. and Mrs. Hurst, left Netherfield just as Elizabeth had predicted.

Confused and heartsick, Jane chose to visit Wapping to get away from her memories of Mr. Bingley. She would care for the Gardiner children while her Aunt and Uncle toured the Lake District.

With her parent's permission Elizabeth had accepted Fiona's invitation for a weekend at Broom Cottage. Miss Feelgood's reputation for creating perfumes and floral scents for ladies was an enticement for Mrs. Bennet to bend the restrictions placed on unmarried daughters.

Elizabeth and Fiona spent pleasant hours tinkering with spells and tossing an assortment of creepy things in the cauldron, which was set on low boil. They had gotten on so well that she had extended her stay, fully enjoying the simple country life.

The days of playing witch provided a temporary distraction for Elizabeth as she found her mind continuously wandering to Mr. Darcy. What was he doing? Who was he dining with? Had he forgotten her? She wished no permanent alliance with the man. Marriage was out of the question because of the difference in their status, but still she kept him at the forefront of her mind.

It would have been good to remain friends with Darcy, since they had magic in common. But their social status being worlds apart, it was not to be. He ran with royalty and she ran with the wind.

Truth be told, Mr. Darcy lacked a certain degree of the tenderness Elizabeth required in a friend. She determined not allow herself to think of him again. At least not for the next five minutes.

It had been a fortnight since Darcy had accompanied the Prince to London. Elizabeth was settling in to a domestic routine at Broom Cottage, and found herself to be much happier living the life of a country witch. The quietude of the magic cottage had much to be said for it.

Wearing an apron over her garden dress, she gathered herbs and returned to the kitchen to begin making bundles of memory-fog sachet. She hoped to send a special gift to Caroline Bingley as the woman had watched Elizabeth stir a cup of tea without touching the spoon. It was a mere slip of a spoon, but the snoop had clearly observed it while they were at Netherfield.

Elizabeth was most concerned since Miss Bingley had not remarked on the incident, which seemed out of character for what little she knew of the woman. A gift of memory-fog sachet for Caroline Bingley's unmentionables drawer might be just the thing to wipe her recollection of the spoon stirring itself. Elizabeth would send the gift in Jane's name and promised herself she would be more careful in the future.

Jane decided to spend the summer with Aunt Gardiner in Wapping. It was the seat of witch history and a place where a good witch could feel a part of the British coven, a sense of belonging to something greater than mere spells and incantations.

She had received no correspondence from Jane, but it was not always required as the sisters could read each other at great distances. Elizabeth knew that despite the distractions of the bustling city, Jane could think of nothing but Mr. Bingley and his rude exit from her life. He had not graced the Bennets with at least a personal goodbye.

One day, Mr. Bingley was in Netherfield, close to

proposing marriage to Jane, and the next day a letter arrived from Miss Bingley claiming they had a change in plans. The letter, both bitter and sweet, said they were leaving for London and would not be returning to Netherfield.

One of Elizabeth's magical gifts was the ability to allow people into her dreams where she could learn much about them. When a person is asleep and wandering the world of dreams, their guard is down and they often open their hearts.

Mr. Bingley had recently visited Elizabeth twice in her dreams. Sad-faced and forlorn, he confessed he had vacated Netherfield, lock, stock, and sisters at the insistence of Mr. Darcy.

How dare Mr. Darcy cause the dearest person in Elizabeth's world such pain? She could not help but wish him to be present in the cottage so she could turn him into a lamp with no oil or a door with no knob.

While Elizabeth allowed herself the luxury of the many torments she might inflict on Mr. Darcy, she had no way of knowing he was completely bewitched by her. He had temporarily won the battle with himself and convinced she was much below his station in life, he remained in London at the Prince Regent's side.

A reasonable person could not expect Darcy to ask for her hand as he recalled her family's behavior at the

Netherfield ball. Mrs. Bennet had thoroughly humiliated her family with her loud boasting of Jane securing the affections of Mr. Bingley. She spoke as if the man were some sort of wild game whose head they could now mount on a wall at Longbourn.

Elizabeth had witnessed Darcy's reaction to her mother's bragging, the expression on his face at the time was dark and hardened. The man would dare not draw close to a family with a matriarch possessed of such an ungovernable mouth. Elizabeth was both embarrassed and relieved.

Tristan, Jane's owl, arrived at the Broom Cottage window. He carried a brief note from Jane. Elizabeth tore it open eagerly, and although it contained no actual complaints, there was an underlying sadness and a want of cheerfulness. The very lack of joy in her sister's missive caused Elizabeth to imagine a potion so powerful that Mr. Darcy would be rendered dumb for the rest of his miserable life.

Taking a teaspoon of Forgetful Dust, she folded it in a small piece of brown paper. Then sealing it carefully so as not to have an effect on Tristan, she tied it to the owl's left foot with a short piece of twine, and sent him winging back to Jane. Whether her sister chose to use the dust or not, at least she would have it at hand. Elizabeth was unsure whether the dust would work against true love, but it was all she could think to do to ease her sister's pain.

She returned to separating and tying her herbs for the memory fog, which as every one knows, is completely different from Forgetful Dust. Elizabeth was tying the last sachet packet when she was roused by the sound of the brass doorknocker. Fearing it might be a witch hunter, her heart fluttered briefly.

Arming herself with a rolling pin, she walked to the door and eased it open. So stunned was she that she dropped her weapon to the floor with a thud.

Fitzwilliam Darcy stood on the step, hat in hand, wearing the look of a puppy seeking treats. Reluctantly, she let him in. "I am not alone," she lied. "Miss Feelgood is in her bedroom."

The dimple appeared in Darcy's left cheek. "Then she is possessed of a doppelganger, as I just passed her on the road. She was headed to Meryton and waved me off."

To Elizabeth's utter amazement, he walked into the room as if he were most at home in a humble cottage. She quickly placed a cloth over the herb packets on the table; concerned they would appear to be what they were…a bit of domestic witchcraft.

"How have you been since we last met?" he asked. "Is your health well?"

"It is," she said. "I would ask of yours, but you appear well. How is the Prince Regent? Has he recovered from his transformation?" She wished to divert the conversation from their personal wellbeing.

"Miss Feelgood is a new person thanks to your mother's rose," Elizabeth said. "She has rid herself of Herman's unwanted attention, and she has become more confident that her spells will not go astray."

He sat down on a tiny chair, crossing one leg over the other with his foot bouncing as if possessed. Unable to contain his energy, he stood and walked about the room, his eyes nervously scanning the jars, bottles, and dried herbs that comprise a witch's kitchen.

Elizabeth was surprised at his agitation, but chose not to speak. There were times when you heard more by merely watching. After a silence of several minutes when there was nothing more he could inspect in the tiny cottage, he came toward her in a nervous manner, and thus began: "In vain I have struggled. It will not do. My feelings will not be repressed. You must allow me to tell you how ardently I admire and love you."

At that moment, Elizabeth felt that she might have accidently sniffed the memory-fog, for she did not recall encouraging his affections at all. On the contrary, she had behaved most coldly toward him. On

Darcy's part there was the one incident when in his excitement at solving the riddle he used the word *love,* but that hardly accounted for his behavior today.

Suddenly, he knelt before her. "You must allow me to tell you how ardently I admire and love you," he repeated, his entire being vulnerable.

Had Miss Feelgood cast a love spell upon him? Elizabeth blushed and in turning red, her anger at both Mr. Darcy and herself mounted. This would not do at all.

Encouraged by both her silence and the color rising in her cheeks, he continued. Unfortunately, being first a man of business and then a man of the heart, he addressed those things he felt should be placed upon the table and dealt with before any talk of romance could properly begin. And so inserting his foot in his mouth, he began his proposal.

"You do understand that my mother, Lady Anne Darcy, was a witch of great renown, and I inherited her gift," he said, his face knotting in distaste. "I have only recently accepted the mantle of magic and am reluctantly beginning to understand the responsibilities that come with witchcraft."

Was his obvious disdain aimed at himself for being the son of a witch, or did he expect Elizabeth to understand that as far as witches go, he considered them below his sanctimonious station?

She refrained from speaking.

"I am given to understand that Mrs. Bennet does not know of your skills, but I sense your sister Jane shares some witch-like traits." He waited for her to speak and then thinking she required some explanation, he continued. "From what I have observed of your mother, if she knew of your gifts she would have capitalized on them."

But still Elizabeth did not respond, for she was learning much about this pompous man and the way he perceived others.

Darcy then indulged in demeaning her younger sisters, which remarks were thoroughly on target and not without merit. But still her anger grew for why had he come here? Was it to list the shortcomings of her family? And if he thought to offset his pledge of love by describing her family in the most negative way, then he had the head-butting mentality of a goat.

She glowered at him; a spell coming to mind, she forced it away, only to have it return. It was on her lips before she could control herself. "Gloat. Bloat. Billy Goat," she whispered. Two small horns popped up on Darcy's head, but he continued unaware.

Now despite his pontificating on her inferiority, she could not help but laugh. True, the horns were small but they were noticeable against his inky black hair.

In spite of her dislike for the man, she could not be insensitive to the compliment he had paid her. Fitzwilliam Darcy was one of the wealthiest men in England. He could have any woman he chose and he wanted her, but for what? Surely he was not proposing marriage? If so, this was the worst proposal to ever fall from the lips of a man.

She allowed herself one deep sigh, as she was about to wound the man *and* his ego. This would not be easy but it must be done.

Darcy continued to insult her family and her craft. She thought of both Grandma Pansy and Jane, two of the loveliest of witches. Elizabeth lost all compassion in a rush of anger. She tried to compose herself but it was not easy as the goat horns caught the light coming in from the kitchen window and it was made all the more humorous by Darcy's being totally oblivious.

Standing up and stepping back to study the cool expression upon her face, he hoped that he would now be rewarded by her acceptance of his hand. He had no doubt she would jump at the chance to be Mrs. Fitzwilliam Darcy. For although he spoke with apprehension and anxiety, his expression was one of total security.

He recalled the Prince Regent's queries about Miss

Elizabeth Bennet and her marital state. His majesty had been more than a slight bit interested in her, despite having experienced her while in a rather awkward condition. It was clear the frog prince was infatuated. Darcy must claim Miss Elizabeth before royalty came calling.

Putting the kitchen table between them, but keeping the memory-fog powder covered, she spoke. "In such cases as this, it is I believe, the established mode to express a sense of commitment and shared feelings for the sentiments avowed."

Darcy stared at her lips making her feel most uncomfortable.

"If I could feel gratitude or a sharing of your feelings, I would thank you now. But..." she walked around the table and went nose-to-nose with him, "I have never desired your good opinion, and based on your little speech, you have bestowed it most unwillingly."

She bit her lip, cautioning herself to be gentle for unrequited love is no one's fault. It is as natural as a spring rain. "I would never wish to cause anyone pain. But you have caused great pain to someone I hold dear."

She looked away for the sight of the horns on his head were causing her to giggle, and her giggles were affecting the memory-fog sachets; they began to float off the table. "I must ask, why with so evident a desire of offending and insulting me, you chose to tell me that you liked me against your will, and even against your character?"

Darcy stood there, his mouth agape for he had surely not expected this. He wondered if Elizabeth were perhaps under some un-love spell provoked by Miss Feelgood.

"You know I have other reasons for my anger toward you," she continued. "Do you think that any consideration would tempt me to accept the man who has been the means of ruining, perhaps forever, the happiness of a most beloved sister?"

Mr. Darcy, who was about to scratch the top of his head where the horns had begun to itch, did not move. He fixed his eyes on her face and with no less resentment than surprise, his complexion turned pale with anger, and his mind spun. He struggled for composure, and did not speak until he had attained it.

Elizabeth waited, knowing she had wounded him and feeling conflicted for doing so.

At length he spoke with forced calmness. "And this is all the reply which I am to have the honor of expecting! I might, perhaps, wish to be informed why, with so little endeavor at civility, I am thus rejected.

But it is of small importance."

His words required a response, and so Elizabeth spoke uninterrupted.

"I have every reason in the world to think ill of you. You have acted unjustly and with malice which you cannot, you dare not, deny." She struggled to control her voice while tears of anger forced their way to her eyes. She would not have him see her cry—not for anything in the entire world.

"You have been the principal means of dividing two of the most dear people from each other. You have exposed one to the censure of the world for caprice and instability and the other to derision for disappointed hopes, and you have involved them in the most acute misery. How dare you?"

Elizabeth could tell by the expression on his face that he was completely unmoved by any feelings of regret. He even had the audacity to smile at her with a look of incredulity. She did the only thing she could think of under the circumstances, she blinked twice and his horns grew two inches.

Seeming to feel the tug of growth he raised his hand to his brow but did not touch the horns.

"So you do not deny that you have done it?" she repeated.

With an attitude both cool and collected, he said,

"I have no wish of denying that I did everything in my power to separate my friend from your sister."

Her temper flared and the cauldron in the fireplace boiled over. Could he be any more pompous? She balled her fists to control her powers.

"I freely admit I did all I could to protect my friend from your sister for it was clear to me that your sister's affections did not match those of Bingley's." When she did not respond, he continued. "Your mother made it quite clear that my friend was an acquisition for the feeding and care of the entire Bennet family, and not the object of love."

He searched her eyes for understanding. "How could I not protect my friend? And yet here I stand before you, placing my heart and my assets in the very same position. I am at your mercy Miss Bennet."

A good part of what he said made sense, but it did not make Elizabeth feel any better. "It is not merely this on which my dislike is founded, but on the way you have treated Mr. Wickham. The man, raised under your roof, is driven to seek his fortune as a cat? How can you justify that?"

"I will not attempt to explain as I have no explanation. My mother was a good and wise witch. If she saw fit to put a locked spell upon Mr. Wickham then she had a just reason. He means nothing to me now, as we have rescued the Prince and Wickham has disappeared from his regiment. I would just as soon forget him."

Shaking her head in refusal to accept Wickham's condition, she said, "You must make peace with the man, for he is like one of your family."

"Do not press me, Miss Bennet, for I have not presented myself to you on behalf of anyone but myself. And now I realize I have thoroughly misjudged how you perceive me."

"You could not have made the offer of your hand in any possible way that would have tempted me to accept it. I had not known you but a short time before I felt that you were the last man in the world I could ever be prevailed on to marry."

"And this," cried Darcy, as he walked to the door, "is your opinion of me! I thank you for explaining it so fully. My faults, according to you, are heavy indeed. But perhaps you might have overlooked them if your pride had not been hurt by my honest confession of the scruples that had prevented me from thinking of you as anything more than a pleasant country lass possessed of an odious family."

She realized her chin was quivering and she could not find the words to respond to him.

"My feelings for you were just and natural. I am not

ashamed to have voiced them. Forgive me for having taken up so much of your time. And now that I understand the regard in which you hold me, I shall bother you no longer. Accept my best wishes for your health and happiness."

He handed her a letter, sealed with gold wax and then attempted to put his hat on his head, but the horns were in the way. He reached up, this time feeling them—first one and then the other. "Very clever, Miss Bennet!" he snarled.

Darcy exited Broom Cottage slamming the door behind him.

Elizabeth crumpled into a chair, overcome with tears. That he should have been besotted with her all this time! He was so much in love that despite all his objections he still wished to marry her! She was stunned to have unconsciously inspired such love, but his abominable pride had destroyed any chance they had for happiness. Her prejudice toward his rank and status had also been a hindrance.

She broke open the wax seal and noted the letter was written on royal stationery. The Prince Regent requested the honor of her presence at court for a private dinner next month. It was an invitation she could not refuse—or could she? A simple thank you note from the Prince would have sufficed. She feared a private dinner in the royal palace when she recalled the look in his deep froggy eyes.

At that moment, the cottage door blew open and the memory fog packets scattered in a gust of wind. Darcy stood with the sunlight behind him, the expression on his face unreadable. He had only been gone mere minutes. Now he stomped across the room, picked her up, kissed her, and flung her over his shoulder. In the blink of an eye, they were outside.

Darcy threw Elizabeth over Parsifal's saddle, mounted the horse, and galloped off.

~ ~ ~

The Romance continues in Lizzy's Love Apprentice
Witches of Longbourn series – Book 2
Coming Spring 2016

Please sign up for my newsletter so you will be the first to know of my new releases.

http://secondactcafe.com/barbara-silkstone/

OTHER PRIDE AND PREJUDICE BOOKS BY BARBARA SILKSTONE

Pride and Prejudice by Jane Austen is one of the most popular novels in English literature. Austen's stories were fundamentally comic but also delivered a thump on the head to the traditions that forced 18th century women to depend on marriage as the only road to survival. The Mister Darcy contemporary series stays true to the original characters while bringing them into modern day England.

MISTER DARCY'S DOGS
Book One in the Mister Darcy series

The mysterious Mister Darcy retains the services of dog psychologist Lizzie Bennet to train his basset puppies for an important foxhunt. Despite knowing nothing about fox hunting, Doctor Lizzie takes on the challenge. Assigned to cover the hunt for the BBC is Society Reporter Caroline Bingley, the would-be paramour of Mister Darcy.

Lizzie's sister Jane and Charles Bingley join the adventure and fall trippingly in love as Lydia involves Georgiana in an ill-planned caper. And why is Wickham lurking in the shrubberies?

Available in eBook, paperback, and audio

MISTER DARCY'S CHRISTMAS
Book Two in the Mister Darcy series

Christmas just became a lot more complicated for dog psychologist Lizzie Bennet and her sisters. While shopping in London they find little urchin Annie and her dog Sammy. As a fierce snowstorm takes over the city, the aloof but alluring Mister Darcy invites the girls, including Annie and Sammy, to spend the night at his penthouse. With the best of intentions Darcy asks Annie and her seven siblings to join the Bennet sisters for a quiet Christmas Eve celebration in his London fortress. The skullduggery begins when Caroline Bingley – the villainess Austen fans love to boo – shows up acting the part of the Grinch and Scrooge combined.

Available in eBook, paperback, and audio

MISTER DARCY'S SECRET
Book Three in the Mister Darcy series

The mysterious Mister Darcy enlists the aid of dog psychologist Lizzie Bennet in his secret quest. Lizzie soon finds herself deep in his battle where familiar villains join forces with evildoers to stop Darcy at all costs. Darcy's true feelings for Lizzie bubble to the surface but will her pride let her reciprocate? And what about that peanut butter kiss?

Available in eBook, paperback, and audio

PANSY COTTAGE
Book Four in the Mister Darcy series

Lizzie plots a secret garden wedding for her sister, Jane and Charles Bingley. Can she outsmart Mother Bennet or will the gorgon prevail? With her nerves in high gear, Mrs. Bennet plans the marriage of her eldest daughter. Behind the scenes, Lizzie races against the clock to design a small garden wedding ahead of her mother's over-the-top ball. Can Darcy cart the unsuspecting Mrs. Bennet to the garden ceremony? Will Mr. Bennet cooperate with Lizzie's plans, or does Pansy Cottage still cast a long shadow in his memories?

Available in eBook, paperback, and audio

MISTER DARCY'S TEMPLARS
Book Five in the Mister Darcy series

Darcy shares his secret vow and his bed with Lizzie Bennet in this fifth book in the Mister Darcy series of comedic mysteries. Will Lizzie help Darcy prevent the theft of the legendary Red Rosary? Can Lizzie get even with Caroline Bingley? And who is the mystery lady in Mr. Bennet's life?

Available in eBook and paperback

MISTER DARCY'S HONEYMOON
Book Six in the Mister Darcy series

Under the guise of honeymooning, Mr. and Mrs. Darcy set off to save a quartet of domestic maids being held hostage in London and to return the legendary Red Rosary to the Templars' treasure vaults. Can they avoid Caroline Bingley, evade the sinister men from Rome, and will they ever get to enjoy their honeymoon?

Available in eBook and paperback

Regency Pride and Prejudice

THE GALLANT VICAR

A Regency tale inspired by Jane Austen's timeless classic ~ *Pride and Prejudice.*

Elizabeth Bennet considers the handsome new vicar at Hunsford parsonage to be everything Fitzwilliam Darcy is not. The Reverend Francis Martel is warm, accessible, and has no difficulty showing his feelings for her. Within weeks of rejecting Darcy's offer, Elizabeth finds herself swept up in a tumult of emotions for the vicar. He shares her wit, her caring for others, and the simple life—so she accepts the vicar's proposal. Will Darcy recover from his injured ego in time to intervene in their marriage? And how will he separate the couple—only days before their wedding?

Available in eBook, paperback, and audio

THE RETURN OF THE GALLANT VICAR

Who is the Gallant Vicar, why did he disappear, and why has he returned on the day Elizabeth is to marry Darcy? Can his passion for Elizabeth be driving him or does he hold some darker secret? Will Darcy bring the blackguard down?

I love hearing from my readers!
You can reach me on FaceBook, Twitter, and at the
Second Act Café

https://www.facebook.com/barbara.silkstone
https://www.facebook.com/pages/Barbara-Silkstone-Author/156097004489447
http://www.twitter.com/barbsilkstone
http://secondactcafe.com

Barbara Silkstone is the best selling author of over twenty novels and novellas. Her comedy mysteries feature goodhearted heroines caught up in screwball situations.

Silkstone's popular Wendy Darlin Tomb Raider series has been compared to the writings of Douglas Adams and Monty Python. Her Mister Darcy series of comedic mysteries based on Jane Austen's classic, Pride and Prejudice now includes six adventures.

Barbara Silkstone's Amazon Author's page
http://www.amazon.com/Barbara-Silkstone/e/B0047L8A8W

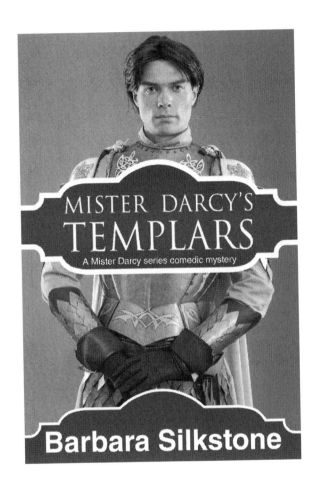

MISTER DARCY'S TEMPLARS

CHAPTER ONE

Darcy and I dashed to the lift in his penthouse foyer with his bodyguard two steps behind us. His resident basset hounds extraordinaire, Derby and Squire, ran between our legs, tripping over their ears and my feet. I clutched Darcy to stop myself from falling.

The elevator doors slid open, and Bingley and Jane appeared as if in a framed photo. I launched myself at my sister and we hugged each other with cries of joy. We had never been apart before, and now Jane was returning from her honeymoon in France as Mrs. Charles Bingley.

Darcy had sent his limo to pick the newlyweds up at Heathrow Airport. They stood before us in the bright light and security cameras of the foyer as a couple—my sister and my new brother-in-law.

I held Jane at arm's length. She still looked like Jane, her long blonde hair with a slight curl at the ends, her bright-blue eyes with long, sand-colored lashes, and yet something had changed. It wasn't her new outfit, although her sleek cream-colored Parisian knit dress was alien to me. Jane left Maidenhead as a girl and returned as a sophisticated lady. Did the words "man and wife" possess some sort of magical morphing spell?

Darcy and Bingley shook hands as proper British gentlemen, then gave up the stuffiness and hugged, performing the guy back-pat ritual. Darcy hugged Jane, and Bingley held me. It felt good and safe and complete to have them home with us.

I glanced up just in time to observe a look pass between Darcy and Bingley. Something was up.

Bingley bent and scratched first Derby and then Squire behind their ears, acknowledging their slobbery greetings.

"Dinner will be set in one hour if that suits you. But please take your time freshening up," Darcy said. "Lizzie and I will meet you in the dining room. If you need anything just buzz Mrs. Reynolds."

Bingley wrapped his arm around Jane and they headed down the corridor to the first guest lounge. Edward the bodyguard followed us to the library where Darcy and I fell into our fireside chairs. The look of relief on Darcy's face told me he had been worried about the Bingleys.

Darcy and I were engaged to be engaged. I carried my commitment to him in a locket worn discreetly around my neck and hidden inside my collar. The little gold heart had once belonged to his beloved grandmother and now held two pictures, one in each half, Darcy and me encased in love.

Time would tell whether Darcy would complete his proposal and I would accept. Being a dog psychologist, I understood the strangled feeling a leash can induce and was in no hurry to officially consummate us since we had been unofficially consummating for some months now.

My world had expanded when I joined forces with Darcy, who was a member of the Knightsbridge Road Templars, a philanthropic society pledged to protecting the glorious history of London. In less than one year I leapt from my humble goal of becoming a psychologist to the royal corgis at Buckingham Palace to being the undisclosed assistant to the richest man in England, not counting the shadowy billionaire figures that populated One Snyde Park, the ritziest international hideout in England and, coincidentally, Darcy's home.

Will Darcy resided in the almost impenetrable fortress as a sentinel, protecting London's history from antiquity thieves and real estate developers. Blending in with those who would have London sell England's soul to sheiks and oligarchs.

Although Darcy found my physical coordination bewildering, he declared my ability to charm to be an asset and for that reason he had begun to bring me along on recent adventures. My main function was to soften the edges of his frequently abrasive personality and convince international billionaires to like us. No problem, because if I used my powers for good, I could be almost adorable.

Darcy stood in front of my chair. I rose to my feet and stepped into his embrace. Our charmed connection allowed us to share our emotions through the slightest touch. He could read me like a much-loved fairytale.

Now I sensed his worry.

"What's troubling you?" I asked.

"Just an uneasy feeling." He grasped my hand, "Shall we await the newlyweds in the dining room?"

We left the library, tiptoeing past Derby and Squire, who snored on the carpet in front of the fireplace.

Although the penthouse was replete with security, Darcy had recently fallen victim to his own trusting nature and become lax in permitting old friends access to his fortress. The guards were now on orange alert and would remain so especially if Caroline Bingley attempted to breach the battlements.

We had just taken our seats when the newlyweds arrived. The four of us sat at one end of the long dining table, the clear glass top allowing any under-table sleight-of-hand or -knee to be seen.

I itched to add a feminine touch to the twenty-three-room penthouse. Was I exhibiting nesting tendencies? Nothing too sissy, but I would love to shave off some of the sharp corners. The indoor park and rock climbing room should remain untouched as they provided the necessary room to exercise, but the master bedroom could use some down comforters and frilly pillows.

The cold steel dining room resembled a James Bond-Blofeld conference room. Hardly appetite-inducing. The first thing to go would be the dining room table I thought as I banged my shin against the cold steel table leg.

Jane had freshened her makeup and run a brush through her hair. I knew her routine as well as I knew my own. I also guessed they were eager to get through dinner and on to their townhome. Honeymooners!

Georgiana was spending the night with a friend and so it was just the four of us, our new family. Odd how time changes the structure of a clan.

Our dinner conversation concerned the sights and sounds of Paris. Although geographically close I had yet to visit the Louvre or the Eiffel Tower. My curiosity about the City of Lights was quickly satisfied by Jane's bubbly account of paintings, vistas, and French cuisine. It was a joy to see her so happy.

Darcy was polite but quiet. Something was nibbling at him and it was not me.

We dined on a light meal of cream of asparagus soup and lobster salad prepared by Mrs. Reynolds, Darcy's talented housekeeper and chef.

"And so was the honeymoon all you imagined it to be?" Darcy asked in an effort to make dinner conversation.

Bingley and Jane blushed a matching shade of pink.

"By their color, they had a grand time," I said, teasing.

Darcy lifted his wine glass in a toast to the couple. "May you always be as happy as you are tonight," he said.

We clinked our crystal and moved on to our orange soufflé dessert.

After dinner we adjourned to the library for a more intimate chat. Darcy had recently installed a sound-scrambler that prevented high-tech eavesdroppers from snooping through the lead-lined walls and windows.

I settled into one of the wingback chairs, Darcy sat on the ottoman at my feet. Bingley and Jane wrapped themselves in a light embrace on the sofa, their digestive drinks standing idly on a side table.

Darcy studied them rolling his snifter of anise, elderberry and Sambuca between his hands to warm it. "I can see on your face the look of a man who cannot hold his tongue one more minute," Darcy said. It was an odd observation since Bingley's face was buried in Jane's golden curls.

"What is on that mind of yours besides your wife?"

CHAPTER TWO

Bingley ceased nuzzling Jane. "You know how it is when you are on your honeymoon, or you will. It is like being drugged on love." He kissed Jane's cheek. "Throughout France, I was oblivious to my surroundings and only on our last night in Paris did I realize someone had slipped a note in my coat pocket, so I am not sure precisely where it was done, let alone by whom."

He passed a folded slip of paper to Darcy, whose brows knotted in a frown as he read it.

Leaning closer, I could see a red cross in the upper right-hand corner. The shape of the cross was identical to the lapel pin Darcy always wore.

Bingley hesitated after giving Darcy time to read the note. "Do you think it's legitimate?" he asked.

"Was this passed to you in Paris?" Darcy asked.

"I am not sure. It could have happened when we visited the Chaalis Monastery. I wish I had paid more attention."

"As you said, old chap, you were on your honeymoon." Darcy read the note twice and then passed it to me.

Carefully I took the paper and laid it in my lap. It was written in a form of calligraphy.

*The Red Rosary is hidden in Temple Church altar.
Beware, there are those who would stop
at nothing to possess it.*

"What does this mean?" I asked.

Darcy raised his hand, palm forward, as if to hold back the tide of my questions. "Not to worry. Thankfully this note is the only negative thing that happened to our honeymooners." The tone of his voice was flip but the look in his eyes said he was concerned.

I lowered my voice despite knowing of the scrambler and asked, "What is the Red Rosary?"

"It is a legend attached to the medieval Knights Templar but not a proper topic for a welcome-home celebration," Darcy said. He dodged the subject by suggesting the fireplace be lit for a romantic setting.

It was July, hot and muggy, but when Darcy clicked the air remote control the room went from air-conditioned cool to chilly and the fireplace flames came on with a poof and a crackle, cozy and romantic. All seemed right with the world and yet something was definitely wonky.

Like a dog with bone, I could not let go. "Please share the story of the Knights Templar and the Red Rosary," I said.

Darcy looked at Jane. "It is violent," he cautioned.

Jane sat erect to deliver her declaration. "I can endure it. I am now the wife of a Knightsbridge Road Templar." She snuggled back against Bingley and he tucked his arms around her.

My sister's brave front was an act. Like most sisters, Jane and I can read each other.

Darcy exchanged a look with Bingley and began, "Our modern-day Knightsbridge Road Templars are nothing like their namesake, the Knights Templar. In the twelfth century, an order of crusading monks was founded to protect the pilgrims going to the Holy Land. They were the original Knights Templar. The ancient Templars became one of the most powerful military orders in Christendom. They were fierce combatants sworn to a strict moral code of poverty and chastity."

"Chastity?" I said.

Darcy smiled, his dimple so delicious I longed to

kiss it but refrained.

"I don't have to worry about you enlisting," I said, with a wicked grin.

Darcy appeared hurt by my remark. Once again I had spoken out of turn.

"Although they spread over much of the known Christian world, they chose to establish their English headquarters in London. They built Temple Church as their base for training in both religion and warfare," Darcy said.

"Didn't they go in search of the Holy Grail?" I said remembering something of their history.

"They did something more practical," Bingley said. "Pilgrims were most often killed for the valuables they carried on their journeys to the Holy Lands. The Templars created a system to protect them from murdering thieves."

Bingley looked to Darcy as if seeking permission then continued. "Before leaving for the Holy Lands, the pilgrims would sign over all their assets to the Templars in return for a letter of credit, in effect a debit card. The letter was encrypted and useless to robbers; but it allowed the pilgrims to draw out money as they journeyed to Jerusalem."

Darcy picked up the thread of the lecture. "Noblemen who wished to join the Templars had to take a vow of poverty. They signed over all their lands as well as their wealth. By deeding their land, castles, and treasures to the Templars, they kept their property from the clutches of greedy King Philip."

I sipped my Sambuca. "Did rulers do things like that? Just take things from their champions?" I asked.

Darcy nodded. "They did then and in most parts of the world, they still do. Many good and noble men went to battle the Muslim sultan Saladin and reclaim the Holy Lands for Christianity. Often these would-be heroes would not return, and so the coffers grew as the Templars legally held ownership of the lands and treasures left in their care," he said. "The Temple Church served as their early depository bank."

Darcy sat on the edge of his desk, his long legs braced, his drink in one hand as he continued to hold me spellbound with his story.

"France was financially on its knees at the time. King Philip had borrowed often from the Templars to keep his kingdom functioning."

Bingley interrupted Darcy, seeming eager to show his knowledge. "Saladin trashed the Templars in the last battle of the crusades, and in disgrace the Templars returned to Europe."

Darcy sipped his drink and cleared his throat. "King Philip saw an easy way out of his obligations to the

Templars. On a Friday the 13th, under orders of Pope Clement, the king's boyhood chum, the Templars were overpowered in surprise attacks throughout Europe. Those that were caught were taken to dungeons and tortured."

Jane and I exchanged looks. The geography and the times might be different, but in our studies we marveled at how evil continues to thrive on Earth hiding under the guise of religion or law.

"On that very same day the Templars were taken captive, all their treasures disappeared, never to be found," Darcy said. "Even the Vatican with their incredible network could not find a farthing. Thus the legends that have arisen around the vanished fortune."

I felt my brow lock in an eye cramp as I studied Darcy. He controlled vast wealth and traveled the world doing good deeds. I often wondered where his money came from. I had jollied myself into believing it was inherited, although he never said it was family money. Now this mysterious note caused me to wonder if Darcy had a connection with the ancient Templars.

Darcy felt my stare and fastened eyes with me. I looked away, worried he would read my thoughts. Trust can be a wiggly worm that is hard to hold in a shaking hand. I believed in the man with all my heart, and yet there were times when two plus two made eight.

I understood from Darcy that he was the Keeper of the Exchequer for the Knightsbridge Road Templars, a neighborhood protection association. But were his modern-day Templars in any way related to the medieval Templars? Half a slice of information was often more tormenting than the entire pie. And my imagination ran away when confronted with just a sliver of pie.

Darcy smiled kindly at Jane. She was the fragile member of our quartet and as such must be cosseted. She couldn't be excluded but we had to be careful in what information we shared with her.

Leaning against the mantel, Darcy kept his eyes on my sister. As he judged her responses he was unnerving me.

"Should I continue?" he said.

Jane nodded looking like a sad rescue puppy.

"The French and Vatican Inquisition team brutally tortured the elderly Grand Master of the Templar Knights, Jacques de Molay," Darcy said.

Jane's hand flew to her mouth to smother a gasp.

"The poor man finally confessed to the most bizarre accusations, including spitting on the cross. That was one of the customary charges one could level during that period. It got a big rise from the crowds," Darcy said, the light from the fireplace reflecting angrily in his eyes.

I huddled my arms around myself, imagining being a hero one day and condemned the next.

"Jacques de Molay recanted his tortured confessions, but because total annihilation was on the king's agenda, the knight was sentenced to be burned alive…slowly," Darcy said, his voice dropping. He turned away, pausing for a moment in his tale.

Jane buried her face in Bingley's shoulder.

Darcy turned back and gave her an apologetic look. "De Molay remained defiant to the end, asking only that he be tied at the stake in such a way that he could face Notre Dame Cathedral and hold his hands together in prayer." He turned again to gaze into the fireplace.

I wondered what Darcy really saw as he contemplated the roaring fire.

"De Molay clutched a Red Rosary in his hands while he prayed. According to legend, he called out from the flames, predicting Pope Clement and King Philip would soon meet him before God."

I perched on the edge of my chair, gripping the arms. "And?"

Darcy took in a deep breath. "The Pope died one

month later, and the king was killed in a hunting accident before the end of the year."

I dropped back into my chair, limp from Darcy's tale.

CHAPTER THREE

"How would the Red Rosary have survived de Molay's immolation?" Bingley asked. "And to suggest that it has been hidden in the altar at Temple Church is folly since the entire building was burned by fire bombs during the German Blitz."

"It just might be the truth. Surviving the burning at the stake would be a true miracle, but think of what the Templars...what the volunteers did during the war. Many artifacts were taken out of London and hidden in the countryside. The Temple Church wooden altar was mercifully in a museum in Durham. God may have been guiding the volunteers."

I reminded myself to breathe as I stared at Darcy trying to understand where my lover left off and the mystery man began.

"If antiquities thieves have marked the Red Rosary for theft then we must confirm its location and secure it. It may now require a more advanced form of technology to protect it. The very rich can afford to structure elaborate thefts, hiring the most brilliant and skilled of scoundrels."

"What's our first move?" Bingley said. He reminded me of Robin jumping at Batman's kneecaps.

"First we discreetly confirm that it truly is in the altar," Darcy said. He switched his gaze from Bingley to me.

I got that uh-oh feeling.

Darcy turned and looked down from the window on to Knightsbridge Road. "Once we know for certain the Red Rosary is in the altar we can outspend, out techno, and completely destroy whoever is planning an assault on Temple Church."

Adrenaline rushed through my body like an espresso with double sugars. I was ready to do whatever it took to protect the Red Rosary even though I'd only just learned of its existence.

"I do *not* enjoy living the life of a sentinel. I watch the billionaire residents who live in the shadows of One Snyde Park. They wait like vultures hungering for an opportunity to take yet another piece of our British history," he said. "No matter the cost, if there is a real assault coming then we must stop it."

Jane was chewing on the inside of her cheek, a nervous habit she had developed in childhood. I shot her a sisterly stare. She stopped chewing.

"It's been a very long day," Jane said, placing the back of her hand against her forehead.

Again Bingley and Darcy exchanged looks. I would have been jealous of their shared secrets but I hoped I would learn more once the newlyweds left.

"Shall we go home, darling?" Jane said to Bingley, standing and tugging on his hand.

Bingley wobbled to his feet.

I thought to lighten the mood. "I do believe, dear brother-in-law, that you suffer from *honeymooner's legs*."

He tottered to my chair and kissed the top of my head. "You, dear sister-in-law, suffer from a fresh mouth."

Darcy let go with a little moan.

I winked at him.

Jane took Bingley by the hand. "I do hope you are revived enough to carry me across our threshold," she said.

"That and more," Bingley said. "That and more."

We walked Jane and Bingley to the lift. The newlyweds were on their way to Bingley's townhouse in the Mayfair section of London, mere minutes away. Darcy buzzed the security guards on the ground floor to alert them to his guests' departure.

Darcy turned his back on our group but I caught him whispering into his communicator. He was assigning one of the guards to stay with Jane and Bingley outside their home for the night.

The little hairs on my arms did their no-no dance.

The lift doors swooshed close. Mr. and Mrs. Bingley were gone.

"We need to talk," I said as Darcy and I returned arm-in-arm to the library.

"Is this a poodle slipper chat?" Darcy said, a tiny dimple showing at the corner of his mouth.

"Slightly poodle," I reached into the ottoman and pulled out the silly poodle slippers I had adopted from Georgiana. They had become my little foot-puppets that found the words I often lost when speaking my heart to Darcy.

I sat in a wingback chair, my slippered feet on top of the ottoman.

"You have given me the feeling that only sinister villains reside in One Snyde. True?" the left slipper-puppet asked Darcy.

The right slipper spoke, "Present company excepted."

Darcy smiled. "This building was constructed for anonymity. The residents are able to come and go from London at will—avoiding all detection. They leave from the tower heliport or via the underground tunnels. One Snyde is the perfect private piggy bank. They hide vast sums of cash, jewels, and designer handbags within their uber-secure flats."

"They keep their fortunes *and* their priceless handbags in their apartments?"

"What better place? A fortified high-rise equipped with uber-secure safes, panic rooms, and guards trained by British Special Forces. A private bank where no one is required to report their holdings to the tax collectors."

I shook my head. "Not even their handbags. What a perfect way to shelter your fortunes. Why invest in art when you can trot out of your flat carrying a purse worth a million or so and no one is the wiser."

"Friday I must attend a Knightsbridge Road Templars board meeting. I would like you to accompany me. I will introduce you as a lady whom I am sponsoring to join the committee. You will appear to be someone interested in historic preservation. They will know you are aware of my activities on behalf of Knightsbridge Road, but I want them to be alert to your safety if you are joining my little team. We protect our own."

"But your society is mostly non-violent, aside from the occasional Russian billionaires. Why should I be in any danger?"

His expression grew scary serious. "The board desires to go against my wishes and permit the conversion of the Down Street ghost station to a nightclub. The funding would come from John Bull and his middle-eastern backers. They are a group without a conscience."

Now I understood Darcy's concerns.

"Bull has promised a percentage of the profits would go to the Knightsbridge Road fund. But there are those who can be bought under the table. Some might pocket the money for themselves. Either way it is a shady situation."

"A nightclub in a ghost tube station hardly sounds appealing," I said.

"There are a good number of reasons why Bull can't be allowed to complete his scheme. The Down Street tube station was one of Churchill's bunkers. It has great historic value. I would sooner post the money myself and have the station rehabilitated into a museum. It should stand as a tribute to the brave citizens of London who sheltered there during World War II and not a place for boozy blokes and subversives."

"You are the head of the Knightsbridge Road Templars. Just say no."

"It is not that easy in a semi-democracy. Bull has

infiltrated our ranks. He has someone in his pocket secretly lobbying for him to get his nightclub permitted. And that is where you come in, my darling Lizzie."

"Me?"

"Your greatest weapon is your apparent lack of guile. Use it well as I introduce you to the members and see if you can discern who is working with Bull while I conduct the meeting."

I shook my head. "Wasn't Bull involved with that Russian who—"

One look at Darcy's face and I felt a shifting feeling near my heart. I stopped dead in my verbal tracks. I could not deny him. What's a little spying for the man you love? Especially when his sister had once been the victim of a kidnapper indirectly related to the chap you were to investigate.

"Believe me, if I thought Bull was permanently in bed with the Russians, he would be long gone," Darcy said. "The buffoon is just a opportunist. But expect him to attempt to win you over."

"I seriously doubt that. The one time we met, I told him I was your personal physician," I said, swallowing a giggle.

Darcy raised one brow, "Would you like to play doctor?"

"Get your mind off the bedroom and into the conference room," I said in a rather unconvincing tone.

My lover smiled and continued with his plan, "John Bull will not be at the meeting but his connection, whoever it is, will inform him of your presence. My personal physician is as good a disguise as any since most of the members will assume we are seeing each other, anyway."

"Seeing each other? That's what we are doing? Seeing each other?"

He stood behind my chair and reached down. "Well, perhaps it is a bit more." He kissed my ear and sent shivers of delight into places the poodle slippers did not reach.

"I would like the Knightsbridge Road team to know of you in case they trip over you or more likely vice-versa," he said, his voice smile-tinged. He touched my cheek with his finger. "I believe I will inform them of your burning desire to protect World War II artifacts. That will best explain your presence."

I nodded as if I understood. For an enigma, Darcy was a great kisser.

"Before Friday, I would like to show you the Down Street Station, including the vintage air raid shelter and Churchill bunker. You have seen only a fraction of the history that lies at our feet."

Fearful of the underground after our recent close call with the Russians and the rodent type rats and cobwebs, I did not look forward to visiting the underground again.

As long as he had confided in me this far, my next question required an answer, but I thought I would pass it to a poodle-puppet.

The right slipper spoke. "Rude of me to ask, but since Lizzie is giving you her heart, as her slippers we have a right to inquire as to your legitimacy. Where does your wealth come from, how do you sustain your lifestyle, and is it legal?"

"I can't believe the audacity of that slipper!" I looked at my right foot in disgust.

"Tips." Darcy smirked. "As a young man I was quite good at waiting tables."

His snarky answer told me he was not about to tell me.

"There is so much for you to learn, if you are still game to assist me. And I promise before I drag you to the altar I will tell you all."

I stood, wrapping my arms around me to keep from the psychological chill that seeped into my bones. This building was a glass hornet's nest swarming with villains.

"Are you ill, Lizzie? You have turned quite pale."

I let a puff of air escape my lips and then nodded. A tour below ground held little appeal and yet if I was to assist Darcy I must meet the rats and rabble.

I scooched out of the slippers and put them back in the ottoman. It was time to rescue Father from his loneliness.

"I've not been back to Pansy Cottage in ages. It is time that I leave for Maidenhead and report that Jane is both home and happy. I'll just be gone a day, not more."

I could feel Darcy watching me.

Wiggling my feet into my shoes, I brushed my palms along my skirt, and spoke. "My dogs and Father await me. I'm off to Pansy Cottage. May I impose on your chauffeur? He should have delivered Jane and Bingley by now." Odd how quickly I had become spoiled. I could so get used to this lifestyle, aside from the panic it induced.

"Let me help you," Darcy said and with one swift move he lifted me in his arms like a baby. "Would you like to reconsider staying for the evening?"

"Um-hum," I mumbled into his chest.

~ ~ ~

Made in the USA
Charleston, SC
09 March 2016